PRINCE OF POT

PRINCE OF POT

Tanya Lloyd Kyi

Groundwood Books
House of Anansi Press
Toronto Berkeley

Published in Canada and the USA in 2017 by Groundwood Books

Groundwood Books / House of Anansi Press
groundwoodbooks.com

We acknowledge for their financial support of our publishing program the Canada Council for the Arts, the Ontario Arts Council and the Government of Canada.

Canada Council for the Arts Conseil des Arts du Canada

With the participation of the Government of Canada
Avec la participation du gouvernement du Canada | Canada

Library and Archives Canada Cataloguing in Publication
Kyi, Tanya Lloyd, author
Prince of pot / Tanya Lloyd Kyi.
Issued in print and electronic formats.
ISBN 978-1-55498-944-7 (hardcover). — ISBN 978-1-55498-946-1 (HTML). —
ISBN 978-1-55498-947-8 (Kindle)
I. Title.
PS8571.Y52P75 2017 jC813'.6 C2016-908207-5
C2016-908208-3

Jacket art direction by Michael Solomon
Jacket design and illustration by Guy Parsons

Groundwood Books is committed to protecting our natural environment. As part of our efforts, the interior of this book is printed on paper that contains 100% post-consumer recycled fibers, is acid-free and is processed chlorine-free.

Printed and bound in Canada

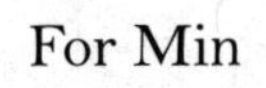
For Min

1

Mom sorts through a basket of fresh-picked herbs, Walt dozes in his chair in the corner of the cabin, and I sit at the table with my homework.

We look like a nice pioneer family, which is fairly ironic.

"There's a druid convention," Dad says, banging his boots against the stoop on his way inside. It's raining a little and his hood's pulled up, a few tufts of brown hair escaping. My dad hurt his back a few years ago. Now he stands with a slight forward bend, as if he's leaning into the wind.

"A what convention?"

"Druids. The whole campground down there is crawling with them," he says.

When I catch Mom's eye, the corner of her mouth twitches.

"Fucking prick," Walt contributes from his rocking chair.

"They're wearing capes, Isaac," Dad says, as if no one in a cape has ever been harmless. "With hoods."

This time when I look at Mom, neither of us can contain it.

"What's so funny?" Dad demands.

"You look..." Mom dissolves in giggles.

It's even funnier because Dad's bushy eyebrows are scrunched together in confusion. In his black rain jacket, standing crooked, with his hair sticking out of his hood, he looks exactly like...

"King of the druids," I say.

That sends Mom off again.

"Bunch of idiots." Dad shakes his head. But he's smiling a little as Mom helps him peel off his jacket and hang it on one of the hooks below the gun rack. "They're going crazy down there. You can hear the chanting halfway up the cut."

He looks at me. "You're going to have to take a trip around the boundary, Isaac."

That's enough to drain the laughter out of me. I let my head flop against the chair back.

Walt opens and closes his mouth over and over again, the way he does every time he tries to say something other than his favorite words.

"Bad feeling," he manages finally.

My grandpa's had bad feelings about everything since his stroke last year. But I admit, I'm no longer a fan of druid conventions, either. I'm definitely not a fan of hauling my ass up and down the mountain for the afternoon. My sister, Judith, used to get this job most often. Now it's me.

"No complaints," Dad says, rapping his knuckles on the table. "This is important."

So I scrape back my chair and throw my sketchbook and a couple of pencils in my pack. Mom tosses me a muffin and a sympathetic look. Then I head out the door.

Straight into Big Bugger.

"Out of my way, beast," I say, pushing against the black fur of his shoulder.

Not too hard, though. Big Bugger has a wicked temper. If he were human, he'd sound like Walt.

Eventually he moves his furry behind, and I manage to get my hiking boots on.

The rain's letting up. Between the treetops there's a bright patch in the clouds where the sun might work its way through. I take deep breaths scented with plant oils and cedar trees, and my irritation gradually melts away as I head south.

Though there's a trail from the access road to our cabin, there are no paths back here. It's government property, not ours, and we take different routes through the brush every time. That way there's no visible connection between our cabin and the grow. If the police ever raided the place, they couldn't prove we knew about the crop.

Not that the police are likely to raid. Dad says they're probably smoking more than they're confiscating these days.

I pick my way around prickly masses of devil's club and through the bracken until I emerge into the sloped, south-facing clearing, where a couple of hundred seedlings reach for daylight.

At first glance the clearing looks as if it's filled with sword ferns. But partnered with each fern is a cannabis plant, roots encased in a burlap sac.

It's only the middle of May. A few months from now, the plants will be taller than I am and no longer so easy to disguise.

I turn my back on the grow and head toward the gurgle of our creek. Then I hop from rock to rock across the water and set off for the southern boundary.

I'll start there.

•

I live on a grow-op. I'm a prince of pot. Future master of a mountain of marijuana.

Even in these days of legalized highs, my family exists on the edge of the law. We're not licensed. We're squatting on government land. And we don't grow a medicinal variety with stable levels of THC. We grow true BC bud. The type that'll get you talking to aliens and communing with your ancestors. Walt and Dad have been perfecting their hybrid for forty years now, and they're famous as these things go. Or infamous, maybe. People call our crop Draft Dodger Dark.

If I were a different sort of person, I could get some saggy-ass jeans, hook a chain to my belt and sell dope from outside an elementary school fence. Or hang out in the back room of a bar like a small-town mafia king.

But I have only one buyer. I sell a bag a month to Lucas, the guy whose locker is next to mine. That's it.

Being the prince of pot is usually the opposite of glamorous. Especially today, when it means a bushwhack through the woods to make sure no random druids are wandering too close to our crop.

After half an hour of clambering up and down ridges, I park myself on a boulder to catch my breath. Below me, an overgrown trail winds through the brush. It leads from the campground beside the highway to a small lake between the peaks to the east. It's rarely used. Just in case anyone ventures this far, Dad and Walt have nailed No Trespassing signs into the tree trunks along the bank where I sit.

I pull out my sketchbook and, once my hand is steady, I try to draw one of the white-pink huckleberry blossoms from the bush beside me. They're so light they float like soap bubbles. My lines seem thick and dark by comparison. A water drop on the petal looks more like an oil drip on my paper.

I'm used to this. Used to my drawings not matching what I see in my head. Used to sitting by myself in the woods, scribbling things. And I'm used to being sent to scout for trespassers. Used to Dad's orders and my grandpa's bad feelings. (Walt doesn't have too many other kinds.) I'm used to steam wisps emerging from the moss as the sun fights its way through the trees.

What I'm not used to — a girl, whistling, walking alone up the trail. The route here is steep as hell, which makes it pretty hard to whistle while you're hiking it. It's also insanely difficult to find, because we like it that way. And this is a well-known bear habitat. More than a little dangerous if you're by yourself.

Walt and Dad tore down the trail markers years ago in favor of extra No Trespassing signs near the base, which this girl has apparently ignored. She doesn't look like the type to be scared of much. She has spiky black hair and wears black-red lipstick, a black tank top and a denim skirt with leopard-print leggings. She should be in a dance club instead of a forest.

"Aren't you worried about the bears?" I don't really mean to say it aloud, but I'm not used to filtering my thoughts out here.

The girl leaps. Both feet fly off the ground at once, as if she's been struck by lightning. Her eyes flick through the trees until she spots me on the bank above the trail.

She smiles then, looking relieved.

"That's why I'm whistling," she says. "So they have time to run away."

Once she's recovered from her shock, she stands with her shoulders back and her chin tilted up at me.

"What if they don't run?" I ask.

"You're Zac, right? Zac Mawson?"

"Isaac, usually." Though I don't mind Zac, the way she says it. I climb off my rock and skid down the moss to stand beside her on the trail.

I know who she is, even though we haven't talked before. Her name's Sam Ko. She's a year younger than me. Moved to town a few months ago.

I glance back at the rock where I've been perched — one of my favorite sketching spots. The sun pierces a stand of birch trees just where a hunk of granite makes a perfectly carved seat.

I've probably sat on that rock for a hundred hours during my lifetime, and not once has a girl walked by.

"It's not a safe trail," I say, turning back to Sam. "There really are tons of bear sightings near here." But I don't want her to turn and hike back down. There's something about the perfect rosy brown of her skin that makes me want to wipe her lipstick away with the edge of my thumb.

"How did you get up here?" I ask.

"My dad's supposed to be off today, but he decided to check on the campground. He dragged me along for the ride."

"Is your dad a druid?"

She grins. "Definitely not. And he's taking a billion times longer than he said he would. I just had to get away, you know?"

I should get rid of her. I should tell her a scary story, or point her in the wrong direction.

"Do you want to see a waterfall?"

Again, not what I should have said out loud.

"You're not scared of the bears?" she asks.

"Not so much."

I take the lead, and she follows close behind. I can feel her eyes on me, which makes me think about how I'm walking, which makes me place my feet awkwardly, which makes me trip on a tree root.

After that, I try to pretend she's my sister. Not entirely effective.

"How do you know this trail?" she asks, when I veer off the main path and through a patch of shoulder-high brush. Twigs tug at my arms and I hold back the biggest branches so she can pass.

"We live near here."

"On the lake?"

"Just up the hill."

No, not on the lake where any passing boat could spot us from the water, or any tourist could pull into the drive with his RV and his overly sensitive nose. We live in a cabin way up the hill from the beach, accessible only by foot. There's a logging road that goes part of the way, then a weed-choked wheel track. We stash our four-wheeler at the top. After that, it's a half-hour hike onto the property.

"Just up the hill" sounds nicer, though. Like we might live in a mansion with a view of the water.

Sam's footsteps stop behind me. When I turn, I find her bending to examine a huckleberry bush. She has one of the blossoms, still shimmering with raindrops, balanced on the tip of her finger.

"Look," she says. "It's like a soap bubble."

I reach down and let another flower rest against my palm.

"I was trying to draw one a few minutes ago and I thought the same thing. Exactly the same thing." Or did I imagine that? "It looks like it could float right off the branch, doesn't it?"

"It's perfect."

After a moment she lets the blossom drop and we continue along the trail. But I'm even more aware of her now. This girl who appears as if by magic, shows no fear of bears and admires huckleberries.

"You sure your dad's not a druid?" I call back to her.

"Quite sure. What about you? You seem like you could be a druid."

I snort. "I've been known to talk to trees. But they don't usually talk back."

It feels like an accomplishment to make her laugh, but I'm glad she's walking behind me so she can't see me flush.

I hear the waterfall before we reach it. When I tell Sam to listen, her eyes widen between her eyeliner smudges.

I feel my face go hot again.

Once we push through the last of the underbrush, we're on the edge of the pool, the waterfall pouring down in a thin, clear arc. Sam pulls out her phone and starts snapping pictures, which is another thing that would make Walt grab his rifle. Good thing he can't get this far from the cabin anymore.

After a few minutes, Sam breaks a granola bar in half for us to share, and I clamber down to the pool for a drink.

"Is it safe?" she asks.

"Nothing above us but mountain."

So she drinks, too. I like that. I like that she takes my word for it.

I've never hiked with a girl from school before. I've never hiked with anyone near my house. Never shown anyone this waterfall since Judith and I found it years ago.

I watch Sam as she stares at the rush of water. She looks softer. When she turns toward me, her eyes are exactly the same color as the water-slicked rocks behind her.

She settles herself beside me on the gravel bank. A woodpecker drums against a dead trunk across the creek, and a chipmunk darts between roots. A branch bobs in the white foam at the back of the pool. The stones glisten and ripple with reflections.

She seems to have forgotten I'm here. She gazes at the water, with a tiny crinkle between her eyebrows.

I can't stop staring. I've never wanted to draw someone like I want to draw her. There's a contrast between the sharp edges of her hair and the round, slightly plump line of her cheekbone.

I ease my sketchbook out of the back pocket where I jammed it.

She stretches. She leans across and plunks her head on my shoulder for a moment — just long enough for me to have a sudden image of turning my face toward hers, but not long enough for me to consider actually doing it.

Then she's up.

"I should get back before my dad goes crazy." She brushes the dirt off her skirt.

I shove my book away.

It's still the most perfect hour I've ever spent on the mountain. I decide this as we hike down the trail, mostly silent, watching our feet on the slick spots.

And I'm an idiot.

Waterfall plus girl. That's apparently what it takes for me to forget where and how I live.

A low, phlegmy grunt reminds me.

Another.

Snuffling.

"Is that what I think it is?" Sam asks, her voice turned raspy. Then she starts whistling. She manages a few notes before she's all air and no sound.

I know the feeling. It's hard to whistle when your mouth's gone dry as a creek bed in August.

That sound was a bear, all right. It was Hazel. I can tell before I catch a glimpse of her cinnamon-speckled fur.

She's going to ruin my perfect hour.

I hear her front paws thump down. She must have been standing on her hindquarters, sniffing the air for us. Now her lumbering footsteps round the corner, branches snapping as she shoves her way through.

I shift a step, so I'm standing in front of Sam. Things will be fine unless she panics.

She grabs my hand. She huddles so close, I can feel her breath on my shoulder.

"Stay calm," I say. "Never look a bear in the eyes. Look down a little, to the side."

Look to the side, talk in a low voice, back slowly away. These are the lessons Dad fed me and Judith with our first venison purees, but these steps aren't necessary with Hazel.

Hazel thinks she's one of us. A huge, hairy human.

"Hey, bear," I say, as Hazel's giant head finally swings into sight.

Behind me, Sam's breathing stops.

2

Hazel plods toward us like a short brown bus, slow and purposeful.

"We got nothing for you," I tell her. "Go home now."

She knows what I mean. And she doesn't like it. Her dark snub nose — a nose I happen to love, most of the time — sniffs itself closer. After three more giant steps, she pushes it against me.

Sam sucks in air as if she's breathing through a straw. That's the only sound out of her, though, which is more than a little impressive.

I shove Hazel's nose away.

"Go away," I say sternly. "Go!"

With a grunt, she drops her head and turns uphill. It's a scramble for her to get up the bank, but she does it, her bulbous butt eventually rolling from sight.

Sam releases my hand and plops herself on the ground. When I turn, she's got her head between her knees. I can hear her teeth knocking against each other.

"Fuck," she says.

I feel a bit like swearing, too. Could she tell that Hazel and I knew each other?

We more than know each other. We're like family. I'm the one who bottle-fed her after Dad hauled her home, a tiny, mewling cub tucked into his jacket. It was early spring, snow still on the ground, and her mother had disappeared. Probably shot by an off-season hunter, Dad said. Hazel's brother was already dead in the den when Dad heard her whimpering. So I fed her, and now she thinks I'm her mom or something.

She even laughs at my jokes. Sort of. When she finds me funny, her giant head bobs back and forth and one paw lifts up and smacks the ground. I bashed my head on a branch last week, and Hazel thought that was hilarious.

I shake my own head as I hunker next to Sam and put a hand on her back.

There's probably etiquette, something you're supposed to do while a girl has a panic attack beside you. I just wait like an idiot, thinking about the smell of shampoo and deodorant and girl sweat, so out of place where everything usually smells like moss.

Thinking about how this is my own damn fault, bringing someone here. If this causes trouble…

"The area's known for bears," I say. "Tons of them." I don't want to say it. I want to tell her to come back and hike here every Saturday. But of course I can't.

"I know about bears. I've just never been so up close and personal before. I should have listened to you," she says. She's getting calmer, slowly. Her breathing has smoothed and she manages a small smile.

"Should we go?" she says.

I offer a hand to pull her up. Once she's standing, she doesn't let go. Tingles run from my palm, up the inside of my arm, all the way to my chest. We start down the trail and every time her shoulder bumps against mine, I notice. Her palm is smooth like water-glossed river rock. When the path narrows and she lets go of me to pick her way through the branches, I immediately start searching for ways to touch her again.

Maybe if I didn't live on the grow, and have fuzzy brown hair and too many freckles, I'd have learned useful social skills. Maybe if I had a life in town and went to school dances or basketball games, I'd know what to do in a situation like this.

About halfway down the trail, as the chanting of druids swells around us, I start to worry about other things. And once my worry arrives, it grows with every step. It grows as the chanting grows.

There are a lot of things you can do if you're a normal guy that you can't do if you live on a grow-op. Date, for example. I've never done that. And I've definitely never hiked to the waterfall with a girl, seen one of our bears and walked the girl out afterwards.

I wonder what Walt would do in my situation.

Then I decide I'd rather not know.

I escort Sam to the very edge of the campground. As we get there, the shadows are spreading and joining, the entire understory of the forest turning to dusk.

When the chanting drops for a moment, I can hear people moving around close by.

I take a deep breath.

"Hey…do you think…." Can girls keep secrets? "Can you not tell anyone about the bear?"

She raises one eyebrow.

"My parents, they're…." I don't want to lie to her, but there aren't a lot of options. "They're big wildlife freaks.

If we tell anyone about the bear, conservation officers will turn up, and that never ends well for the animal."

"They'll shoot it," she says.

And maybe a few others. I nod. "Can we keep it secret?"

She purses her lips and tilts her head to the side, as if she's assessing me, not the question. Then she nods.

I turn to go.

"Hey," she says.

I stop.

"Can we talk about it on Monday?"

"Sure."

With that, she stalks through the last row of trees and into the campground as if she's never had a frightened moment in her life. And I turn back uphill, my legs tired but my mouth stretching in an impossible grin. I can actually feel it pulling the skin of my cheeks.

Hazel didn't ruin my perfect hour after all.

•

When I reach our cabin, Dad's sitting on the front steps smoking his pre-dinner joint, his eyes relaxed and his cheeks ruddy with sun. Hazel rests on her haunches near his side. Big Bugger lounges nearby.

I find myself arranging the scene to fit on a canvas, mixing the brown that captures his hair and picks up in Hazel's fur and the flecks in the branches above him.

Mom says I look just like him.

"What took ya so long?" Dad says.

I've been considering this question all the way up the trail.

"I found a hiker along the south boundary. Had to head her off," I say.

With Dad, it's always better to tell the truth. You don't have to tell the whole truth, but he can smell an outright lie the way he can smell a whiff of mildew on a handful of bud. He'll gaze at me with brown eyes full of compassion and disappointment, and it will feel as if he's stabbed me.

"Hiker? By herself?"

I nod.

He grunts.

Dad's not big on communication. He talks during Sunday services, he talks to Mom, and he talks to the bears. That's about it. Unless I start meeting more girls in the woods, I might end up like him.

"She coming back, Isaac?" he asks.

I hope so.

I force a chuckle. "She caught a glimpse of Hazel through the trees. She's not coming back anytime soon."

With another grunt, Dad hauls himself up. He gives Hazel a rub on the head before he turns inside.

"Wash up," he says over his shoulder. "Dinner's almost ready."

I head to the rain barrel beside the house to slosh a few ladles over myself. But not before I catch Hazel's gaze.

Sure enough, her big head is swinging side to side and her paw's stomping.

I may be wrong about that bear not being human.

There are five bears around the grow. There's Hazel, the smallest and by far the most tame. Big Bugger is huge and ornery, but tame in his own way. The other three are less predictable. The twins are two years old, still playful, and stupid enough to take half your head off with a swipe if you're not careful. Queenie is an old female who tends to sit at the edge of the clearing and look down her nose at the rest of us. She's the least tame of the bunch, though she's been around since I can remember.

Dad traps some smaller animals, which he tosses to the bears. A few times a year, he takes down a deer, though that's been harder since his back started bothering him. I haul a massive bag of dog food up the trail every few weeks. The rest of the time, the bears look after themselves.

Except for Hazel.

As I head inside for dinner, she settles by the door to wait for her scraps.

At the table, Dad has opened his Bible. He looks deep in concentration. When Walt lets loose a volley from the corner, Dad doesn't even flinch.

My grandpa's been causing problems. Though I haven't been home all afternoon, I can tell by the tightness behind Mom's smile as she kisses me on the cheek. That, and the string of muttered curses coming from Walt's chair. If there were a world championship of swearing, Walt would win gold, hands down.

"Fucking prick fucking prick."

Our cabin is what you might call rustic. There's only one main room — kitchen table, a few chairs, Walt's bed along one wall. Before Judith and I were born, Dad added a loft for himself and Mom. Later he built a lean-to off the side for my sister and me. Now it's just mine.

We have cold running water piped from the creek, and an outhouse at the back. There's a small generator if we really need it, but since we have to haul fuel up the trail jerry-can by jerry-can, we save the electricity for emergencies and special occasions. A few years ago, Judith started complaining about hygiene, so Dad and I rigged a summer shower outside, with hoses spiraled on the cabin roof to heat the water.

Overall, our place isn't bad, considering that it's basically a fort in the woods.

"Fucking prick." Walt leans forward in his chair and glares at the room.

We could use a little more soundproofing.

He's not cursing at anyone in particular. And you'd think, after all this time, I could let his words roll off me. But the way Walt produces them, like blasts of venom, they hang in the air. Mom's shoulders tense and she sucks a breath between her teeth. The words don't roll off her, either.

"Is it too late for a break?" I ask. "I could take over."

She's stirring a handful of nettle leaves into a pot of stew on the woodstove. Some of her dark hair has escaped her braid, and her long thin fingers look frail on her spoon. I feel a stab of guilt.

Almost always, Mom heads out for a walk in the late afternoon while I keep an eye on Walt. She spends most of her time picking medicinal plants, which she mixes into Draft Dodger Dark teas — another infamous family product. But thanks to my gallivanting down the mountain and back today, I've sucked away her time.

Her head's bent over the stove, and I have to lean down to catch a glimpse of her face. The circles beneath her eyes.

She bumps her shoulder against mine and shakes her head.

"Don't you have homework?"

"Already done."

"Well, then. You can set the table."

While I plunk down spoons and bowls, I think about Sam saying she needed to escape for a while. That's why she came up the mountain. To escape.

It's not exactly an option for me. If I disappeared, Mom would be caught between Dad's silence and Walt's ranting. Plus I'm the only one who goes back and forth to town anymore. How would they get supplies, arrange meets, sell our product? It's not that I do hours of work around here, but I'm the grease that keeps everything moving. Especially this past year, since Judith moved into town.

I understand why Judith went, but Dad took it as a personal betrayal. I'm not sure he could handle it if I left, too. Maybe only one person in each family is allowed to escape.

I wouldn't leave anyway. I can't imagine waking up anywhere but the lean-to, with branches brushing against the roof and birds going crazy in the trees and Hazel waiting patiently outside. I could never live in a city full of crowds and traffic.

"Isaac? Your dad's ready to say grace." Mom's looking at me. While I've been standing here mulling, gripping the last spoon, everyone else has sat down. Even Walt.

So I slide the spoon quickly into place, plop myself into a chair and bow my head while Dad says the prayer.

After that, dinner goes downhill.

Grouse stew is a favorite of mine, and I'm as hungry as one of the bears at feeding time, but Walt barely pauses for breath between cussing and chewing. I can tell Mom is trying to hold her smile. She asks Dad about the druids.

None of us can hear his answer.

"Fucking prick," Walt says, a dribble of gravy running from the side of his mouth. Mom reaches over to wipe it, but he bats her hand away.

Even though Walt is as gray and wrinkled as a seed pod in winter, the guy's strong. Wiry. I wouldn't want to cross him.

We eat fast, and we're mostly done when Mom nudges me. I follow her gaze to Dad. With his head propped in one palm, he's almost asleep over his bowl. That one joint a day eases his back pain enough for him to sleep, but sometimes it kicks in a little early.

Walt sees us looking, and he chucks his spoon across the table.

"Fucking prick."

Dad's eyes snap open as he pulls himself upright. He doesn't say a word to Walt. Just goes back to scraping up his last bites of meat, the way I am.

Walt was never the kind of grandpa you read about in books. He did half a tour in Vietnam in the seventies as a rear helicopter gunner. That sort of thing doesn't equip you for story time or baseball practice.

He had the stroke last winter. At least, we think it was a stroke. Mom and I found him slumped in his chair, mouth sagging to one side, and it was weeks before he could get around the cabin again. Since then, he's able to speak, but only slowly, and it takes patience to understand him. Mostly, he sticks with the cursing.

"Prick," he spits.

Dad throws his spoon into his empty bowl, where it clatters against the rim. He shoves his chair back.

"Going to feed the animals," he says on his way out.

"I'll do dishes," my guilt tells Mom. "You can get out of here."

She shakes her head and kisses me on the temple. Then she clears the plates while I fill tubs from the pot warming on the stove. One tub for washing and one for rinsing.

"How come I always wash and you always dry?" I whisper. I whisper so we don't disturb Walt, who's nodded off without leaving the table.

"So you don't snap me with the towel," she says.

I snap her with the dishcloth instead, which sends drips flying and prompts a squeal from Mom and a startled snort from Walt.

"Sorry," I whisper. But she's smiling now, so I'm not really.

I wait while she dries the last plate, then we both slide out the door.

The sky's blue-black, still fighting off darkness with the last of its late-spring strength. In the dusk, I find Hazel in her usual place beside the steps, her tongue pushing an empty bowl back and forth. She's the only bear I can see. They probably followed Dad somewhere for their feed. Those animals would follow him anywhere.

Mom takes a deep breath as she settles herself beside me on the top step.

"Your grandpa was in fine form this afternoon," she says. Which is her way of saying he was acting like Big Bugger with a thorn in his butt.

I think of my own afternoon with Sam at the waterfall. It felt like I was in a whole different world.

A bat swoops between the trees, navigating blindly and perfectly. Then Dad's shadow crosses slowly toward us, his untucked shirt flapping a little in the breeze.

Dad's not the best in groups of people. He doesn't go to town much anymore. To him, town is as foreign as life in our cabin would be to most people. Here, though, he's perfectly at home. He walks through these trees as if nothing could hurt him, ever. As if he were born here.

Which he was.

"Time to head in," he says when he reaches us. He ruffles my hair a little, as if I'm still a kid, then lets his fingers trail over Mom's shoulder.

"You go ahead. Walt's asleep, and we'll be right behind you," Mom says.

We sit and watch the trees become black silhouettes on an almost-black sky. The stars pop out, handful by scattered handful.

Mom sighs beside me.

"I started to wonder, when you were so late this afternoon," she says.

I shift uncomfortably. "Had to scare off a hiker."

For a moment, I imagine telling her about Sam. I want to explain the feeling I had at the waterfall today, wanting to draw Sam like I've never wanted to draw anything before. Or I could describe what it felt like to touch Sam's skin. Like the shock you get from glacier water, without the cold.

But the words won't come out.

Maybe some of my confusion overflows into the night air, because Mom reaches over to pull my head against hers.

"I worry about you sometimes," she whispers.

"I'm okay. I'm always okay."

She plants a kiss on my temple.

I wish Judith were here. My sister wouldn't just smile, then turn inside. She'd lean forward a little until she caught my eyes.

"What's going on?" she'd ask.

A gust of wind sweeps down the mountain, pushing the branches against one another.

I have no idea how I'd answer.

3

All the way to school on Monday, I think about Sam.

I imagine weaving through the press of bodies in the school hallway until I find her. In one scenario, we pass and share a quick smile. I breathe a waft of girl shampoo before she disappears. In the other scenario, she sees me and all conversation with her friends stops. She stares as I grow closer. Her friends part like the Red Sea. My arm wraps around her waist. I press her against the lockers, and I kiss her.

I'm guessing that one's less likely. It sure makes the drive go fast, though.

In the end, I don't have to scan the hallways. As soon as I pull into the parking lot, I spot her leaning against the cinder blocks near the side door of the school. Today she wears cut-off shorts. Her lips are a shiny bubblegum-pink. A silver twist that looks like a fishhook dangles from one ear.

I'm wearing jeans and a gray T-shirt, the same thing I was wearing Saturday. This didn't seem like an issue until now.

It doesn't matter. As she smiles at me, I feel my own grin spreading.

"I've been asking around about you, Zac," she says when I reach her. She turns toward the doors and I follow her inside, into the orange-tiled foyer that echoes with the morning energy of crowded bodies. We push through clouds of hairspray and perfume, floor wax and disinfectant, gym shoes and — once — a waft of pot.

"Asking about me?" I have no idea what people would say. They'd probably have to squint and wrinkle their foreheads to remember who I am. "What did you learn?"

"That you're a good artist but you're not serious about it, and you're a bit of a freak."

A snort escapes me. Creston is a live-and-let-live kind of place. I doubt anyone spends a lot of time analyzing my life. But it's interesting to know that this is their conclusion.

I shake my head.

A group of teachers passes us, leaving ripples of coffee fumes and cigarette smoke.

"Hey, I'm just repeating what I heard," Sam says, bumping a shoulder against me. "I have to say, you didn't strike me as a *complete* freak."

"What are the qualifications, exactly? Is there an application form?"

Sam presses her lips together like she'd rather be too cool to laugh, but one bubbles out anyway.

"What I'm trying to tell you," she says, pulling me toward the courtyard in the center of the school, "is that you seem okay to me, and you carry a sketchbook. You don't seem like someone who's given up art."

After the press of the hallways, the courtyard's plank benches and evergreen shrubs seem like a miniature forest.

When I'm painting, even if it's just in art class, I feel as if the brush could take over my whole self. As if I'm someone else, someone I don't even know yet. The most frustrating thing about living on the grow is not having access to art books or websites or after-school classes. I struggle along by myself most of the time. But giving up painting isn't an option.

If I explain all that, I really *will* sound like a freak.

"I stick to myself," I say.

"And perfect your art in solitude, so you'll become famous after your death?"

"Exactly." It's not the worst life plan.

When we sit on one of the benches, she twists to face me. Her knee touches my thigh, though she doesn't seem to notice.

I notice.

"So you're not a freak, Zac."

"No." Maybe.

"But you quit painting."

"I didn't quit. Mr. Pires entered me in a contest without me knowing, and I won. But I didn't accept the prize."

"How come?"

"Is this an interrogation?"

She laughs again. "Are you avoiding the question?"

"The prize was to have my painting printed in a magazine. Their writer was going to visit me and do a profile. But I was busy. My grandpa was sick."

That's not why I couldn't have the canvas published. I'd painted our cabin. Our front stoop with the weathered logs above, the hemlocks standing guard and the mountain peak rising over it all. Anyone around here — anyone who hiked, at least — could look at that peak and figure out approximately where our cabin lay.

I was an idiot to ever paint that scene.

"One magazine interview doesn't seem like a big commitment," Sam says.

She has no idea.

"Maybe my art isn't meant for magazines."

"What's it meant for, then?"

Which is a ridiculous question. "It's meant to exist."

She furrows her eyebrows.

"The ways trees exist," I say.

"You're a strange dude, Zac Mawson." She shakes her head. "But I like you anyway."

I like you, too. I like the way you throw everything into the open.

I only manage these words inside my head. Though she's shifted her knee away from my leg, I can still feel a circle of heat on my skin.

The bell rings. For the first time, I notice a gaggle of girls pressed against the glass of the courtyard, watching us. They're Sam's friends, waiting and giggling.

I have class.

"Do you want to…" How can this feel so awkward? "Do you want to get lunch together?"

Sam's shiny lips curl into a pout. "Can't. We're doing a drama skit this afternoon and we have to practice." She nods toward her groupies.

Of course she's the drama type. I should have known.

"Tomorrow?" she asks.

"Okay."

She pops from the bench and bounces over to her friends, leaving me in a cloud of bubblegum pink.

•

My truck rumbles along the ruts in the dirt road that cuts through the orchard toward my sister's place. This is where I usually spend my lunch hour.

Judith lives in a converted old school bus that my dad bought for cheap. It still has the traditional yellow paint job, but the original owners turned the emergency exit at the back into a real door. Inside, it's like a small RV, with wooden cabinets and orange upholstery. There's a loft bed above the driver's seat, a table that folds down into a second sleeping space and even a miniature bathroom. The bus is parked in a perfect spot under the apple trees, on a lot Dad owns a few minutes from town. He's even rigged electrical and water hook-ups.

Today there's a flashy blue Mazda on the grass between the bus and Judith's beat-up Honda. Then I spot the guy who matches the car, standing on the plastic stool that serves as Judith's front step. Judith's in the doorway, one hand playing with the hair at the nape of his neck.

He's a decent-looking guy, though short. He's wearing a golf shirt and dark jeans that seem as though they may have been ironed.

As I climb from my truck, he steps onto the grass, reaching out a handshake.

"Hey," I say, keeping my voice neutral.

"Garrett, this is my brother, Isaac," Judith calls from the doorway.

We shake. He uses too much cologne and there's something weasel-like about him. The longer I look, the less I like him.

"Garrett's on his way to work," Judith says.

"Called in sick this morning," he says. Then he winks at me.

I cringe.

He looks back at Judith. "I'll see you later."

"I might be busy," she says with a flirty smile I've never seen before.

"You're working tomorrow, aren't you? I'll come by the bar."

Without waiting for her answer, he heads for his car.

"See ya, bud," he says as he passes.

As he backs around my truck and then quickly down the drive, Judith turns inside. She emerges a moment later with her hands wrapped around a giant coffee mug. Then she leans back in one of the old lawn chairs at the side of her bus.

"Hey, handsome," she says as I flop into the chair next to hers. The vinyl creaks under my weight, but it holds.

Even in her sweatpants with her hair unbrushed, my sister is drop-dead gorgeous. When she was in tenth grade, a talent scout spotted her in the crowd at the Blossom Festival parade and gave her a card for a modeling school in Vancouver.

You can imagine what Dad and Walt said about that. The words "devil's work" were used multiple times.

I don't think Judith really wanted to go anyway. She's like me. Solitude's in her bones. She has to work at the crowded bar, but other than that she spends her days here in the orchard. Monday evenings she takes a couple of first-year psychology classes at the community college.

"I brought you home a cheeseburger last night. It's in the toaster oven," she says.

That's a perk of her hotel work.

"What about you?" I ask.

"I'll have something later."

The door's propped open, but I smell him anyway as soon as I walk in. Sex, plus whatever crap they put in men's perfume, plus a trace of cigarette smoke. It almost makes me gag.

I grab the burger, shake the burn off my fingers and head back outside.

"Rough night?" I ask.

Judith has her head tipped against the lawn chair, eyes closed in the sun.

"A good night," she says.

"Oh, yeah? How good?"

When she doesn't answer, I reach over to give her shoulder a shove.

"Spill," I say, around a giant bite of burger. I may as well figure out what I'm dealing with. Get to know the enemy.

"He works at the brewery, but not on the line. Some office job. I met him in the bar a couple of weeks ago."

Maybe it's evolutionary brother-instinct that makes me distrust the guy. I mean, I'm in favor of Judith having fun. But not with Garrett from the brewery. She deserves better.

She pokes my arm. "Stop making that face. He's a good guy."

She deserves great.

"I might have met someone, too," I tell her. I say it mostly to change the subject, but then I find I can't look at her. I have to stare at my burger, picking the last few sesame seeds off the bun.

"Oooh!" She immediately swivels toward me, tucking her feet up on her chair. "Tell me more."

"You'd like her." And suddenly, the stink of that guy is gone in the pleasure of telling Judith about Sam. I tell her everything. She howls when I get to the part about Hazel. She almost falls off her chair.

"Why can't we just be normal?" she asks, once she can breathe. "Why do we have to protect our future dates from rampaging bears?"

I shake my head.

"Do you know people can actually be scared to death by bears? It happens if too much cortisol gets into their blood," she says. "Happened to a kid in Vermont. I read about it in one of my psych articles."

"Sam didn't die," I say.

"You didn't introduce her to Dad, obviously."

"I told him there was a hiker."

"But not that the hiker was hot." My sister grins.

"I may have neglected to mention that."

"Bring her by sometime. Soon! I want to meet her."

"I will," I promise. Then it's time to get back. I give Judith a quick hug before I climb into my truck. With my arm over the back of the seat, reversing down the long driveway, dodging apple trees, I'm grinning again.

I've never smiled this much before.

•

When Judith was thirteen, she launched a massive campaign to stop homeschooling and attend real high school. Creston has a few tiny elementary schools which all feed into one central high, grades eight through twelve. Judith wanted in on the action, even if it meant hiking down the mountain and riding the puke-scented lake-road school bus each morning.

She won that battle, and I followed in her footsteps when I hit eighth grade. But every time the subject came up, Dad reminded us we were in school on one condition.

"Keep your head down."

I've followed that rule religiously. I'm the guy no one's going to recognize in the yearbook.

So I'm a little surprised when I walk through the double doors of the school after lunch and one of the guys from the basketball team shouts, "Isaac — you the man!" and raises his hand in what turns out to be a high-five, though I don't realize this until awkwardly late.

He doesn't hang around to explain himself.

On my way down the hall, two girls stop talking, watch me pass, then resume talking twice as fast.

There's a hole ripping through my gut, like I've been sucker-punched.

As I'm dumping my stuff in my locker, Lucas shows up at the locker beside mine.

I wouldn't exactly say Lucas and I are friends. It's more that we're alphabetically close. We've shared hallway space for the past few years. Thanks to a lapse in judgment when I was thirteen, and the need to buy some protection for my awkward homeschooled ass, I sell him pot.

He's abnormally tall, with cropped brown hair and wire glasses. He wears jeans and striped T-shirt variations every day, along with a butt-ugly green track jacket.

"Is something going on this afternoon?" I ask. If there is, Lucas will know. The guy's a mechanical genius, so he spends plenty of time in the school shop. But he's aiming for med school, too. He's a strange sort of social chameleon.

"Not for thirty-eight more days," he says.

"What happens in thirty-eight days?"

"Graduation, man." He raises his palms, as if clouds are parting and the heavens opening. Then he narrows his eyes. "Why do you ask?"

"Somebody high-fived me on the way into school."

At that moment, another group of guys walks by.

"Hey, it's Grizzly Adams," one calls.

I have no idea what that means, but I swear he's looking straight at me.

"See?" I ask Lucas once they've passed.

"Odd," he concedes.

All the head-over-heels puppy-love feeling has leaked out of me. Still, it's too early to jump to conclusions. That's what I tell myself. I'll wait until after school. I'll wait until I talk to her.

Once the bell rings, I spend an hour in English, thinking about *Julius Caesar*. Then I drip paint in art.

If it weren't for art, I'm not sure I would bother with high school. It's not as if *Julius Caesar* is going to prove wildly applicable to my grow-op career. But art — the class is a complete escape. An hour goes by like a minute, and I've thought of nothing except color and texture. This particular canvas already has greens running diagonally down the bottom half. Today I add shades of mountain blue at the top. I plop dollops of paint, then choose just the right angle and watch gravity do the work.

"Impressive," Mr. Pires says.

Though he lives in town, Mr. Pires looks as if he could run his own grow. He has bark-brown skin and thick, curly black hair that he wears in a ponytail. He dresses in classic rock T-shirts with lab-coat smocks over top.

Once he moves on, I add a couple of smaller dots of purple and let them run as well.

They run farther than I intend.

Because when I say I've been thinking about *Julius Caesar* and acrylic paints all afternoon, that's a lie. I've been thinking of these things against background images of Sam Ko.

As soon as the bell rings, I scan the hallway for her.

A couple of girls find me first.

"I can't believe what you did," one gushes, linking an arm through mine.

"Are you, like, some sort of animal whisperer?" her friend asks.

These girls are both blonde. I've seen them around, but I can't find their names inside my brain. Possibly my mind has been flooded with pheromones.

"Was it a black bear or a grizzly?" the first one asks.

There it is. I can't deny it any longer. My feet stop moving. My gut clenches up, then my chest, then my throat.

The girl drops my arms. "What did I say?"

That's when I spot Sam, finally, in a pink slouch hat that matches her bubblegum lips. I glare at her.

When she sees me, her eyes widen.

"I can explain," she says.

The blonde girls melt away as Sam grabs my arm and pulls me toward the courtyard.

I shake off her hand. "You told everyone?"

I have to talk through clenched teeth or I'm not sure what will come out of me. I try to remember that to a normal person, this is probably no big deal. She doesn't know that Hazel's like family. She doesn't know that I live on a grow-op. How would she even imagine that either of those things could be true?

So I try. I try to be normal and let her know that I'm unhappy without going all backwoods about it. But I can't remember ever feeling this pulsing, can't-think-straight fury that wants to explode from me.

She can obviously read it on my face.

"I told two friends," she says. "And they're both completely trustworthy. Wouldn't tell a soul. But then we were talking about it in the foyer at lunch and someone overheard, and then I had to repeat the whole story, and..."

What pops into my mind, ridiculously, is *Et tu, Brute?*

I can't say that.

"They won't tell anyone else," Sam says. "I'll make sure."

This isn't her fault. That's the worst part. I could have foreseen it the minute I spotted her on the trail and chose *not* to scare her away.

I did this.

My teeth still clenched, I suck in a deep breath.

"I'm glad you got home safe on the weekend," I tell Sam.

Then I walk away.

What did I think was going to happen? Did I think I could have two separate lives, one full of bubblegum and milkshakes and the other laced with THC?

I *did* think that, temporarily, which makes all the words Walt has ever spit at me uncomfortably true.

Sam calls my name as I leave the courtyard, but I don't turn back.

4

Dad's cleaning the Winchester 94 while he talks to Mom. As I take off my jacket, the word "druid" catches my attention.

I make myself a sandwich, then lean against the counter to listen.

It seems that when the attendees of the druid convention packed up their mushrooms and their robes, one stayed behind. In a tree. Mom ran into him on her most recent herb-picking expedition.

"The campground attendant must think he's harmless," she says, shrugging.

"How the hell did he get a treehouse built?" Dad asks.

"Most of it looks old. He'll be lucky if he doesn't crash through the floorboards in the middle of the night."

Dad doesn't say it out loud — that would hardly be Christian — but I can tell what he's thinking. We'll be lucky if the druid *does* crash through the floorboards.

"I only talked to him for a few minutes. He said he was communing with the spirits of the forest."

"Fucking prick," Walt adds from the corner.

Dad has the Winchester back together. He sets it in place on the rack above the .30-06 Springfield, a moose-hunting rifle also ideal for scaring the pants off ganja thieves. And possibly druids.

My parents let the conversation drop, but we all know how the issue will end. Dad will drop a hunk of meat at the base of the druid's tree in the middle of the night and leave Big Bugger and another bear or two to scare him straight down the highway.

That's how we keep things balanced in the woods.

It would be good if life was as clear in the outside world.

•

As far as I can see, high school was never meant to be fun. It's full of cinder-block walls, tired wardens and inmates who would rather be anywhere else. If you gave them a chance to escape into the woods and not come back, half these kids might make a run for it.

Then there's me. I'm the one with the choice. When I leave school and dedicate my life to the tender propagation of high-yield marijuana, my parents will not only understand, but applaud. They'll praise my dedication and loyalty. I'll be following in the family footsteps.

I could ditch class forever, if I wanted to.

But on Tuesday morning I get up while it's still dark outside, I wash in freezing water, I push past the bears crowded around my front door, and I hike through the morning's spiderwebs (webs that always seem to be built exactly at the level of my face). Then I drive to this pasty place, where everything's painted beige and no one knows me.

I do this...why? To flirt with an untrustworthy girl? To pretend I'm a friend of the guy whose locker is beside mine, when I know barely anything about him? There is no possible reason, except that I have art today and I feel as if nothing will be right again until I'm holding a paintbrush. So I walk through the hallway as if it's my own personal endurance test. When someone's shoulder bumps mine, I take a deep breath and keep moving. When a ham sandwich arcs overhead and splats onto the floor to cheers from a group of ninth-grade boys, I sidestep the mustard. I keep my head down until I reach my locker.

My pink and purple locker.

The word SORRY is scrawled across the metal in some sort of waxy substance. It's written in big pink letters in the middle, then repeated in miniature purple versions all around the edges.

I touch a glob with one finger.

Lipstick.

As my face flushes its own cosmetic shades, I stomp to the bathroom and grab a handful of paper towel. When I get back, a few people are giggling.

Lucas arrives. "Whoa," he says. "It's like Valentine's Day puked on you."

I ignore him, swabbing at the first letters. The lipstick smears into an oily mess, and soon there's a softball-sized lump of paper in my hand and still a pink-and-purple film on the metal.

Lucas finishes organizing his stuff and shuts his locker so he can lean against it.

"Shouldn't this be a good thing?" he asks.

I pause to stare at him. "How can it be a good thing?"

I walked away from Sam in the courtyard because she was too loud and just plain too much. She thought vandalizing my locker would help?

Lucas doesn't answer, so I wave my purple paper wad at him.

"Why would she do this?"

"A girl who writes apologies in lipstick…I think someone looooves you."

"This is supposed to be a mating ritual?"

I scrub away the final smear, chuck the paper at the garbage can near the classroom door, then open my locker to dig out my books for first period.

A construction-paper heart has been stuffed through my locker vent. It flutters toward me.

The bell rings. I slam my locker door and follow Lucas into homeroom, my binder in one hand and the heart in the other. I'm convinced that every single person in here is smirking at me. Even the teacher.

As I slide into the desk beside Lucas, I can feel him silently laughing. I know that he's laughing at my reaction more than he's laughing at the lipstick. To him, a smeared message on a locker is probably no big deal. But Lucas doesn't understand how ingrained my invisibility is.

Sam definitely doesn't understand. I'm in school on the condition that I don't attract attention. That no one stops to wonder who I really am, or why my parents never turn up for parent-teacher night, or why I wear the same three shirts in rotation, probably with a whiff of pot attached.

What if everyone starts asking questions, beginning with my purple locker and ending with my pot sales and pet bear?

The PA speaker crackles to life as I finally manage to get my heart rate back to normal.

"Wait!" Lucas's whisper stops me as I'm crumpling the heart. "There's a note."

I smooth the paper and look down at the round curvy letters.

It's the worst poem ever.

Oh, the girl from the town was so sad
When the boy from the forest was mad
That she promised she would
From then on be good…

Lucas reaches over to snatch it from my hand.

"Hey!"

I grab for it, but he extends his arm to the other side, holding it out of my reach. It doesn't matter, though. I can read the last line.

Except if he wanted her bad.

"Something to share, Lucas?" Ms. Aloni's voice is too sharp and crackly to be real. It's like an actor's impersonation of a teacher's voice.

Lucas, thank God, crumples the heart in his hand.

"Nothing."

She hovers over him, lips pinched even more tightly than usual. I can see she's deciding whether to force him to hand over the paper.

"Ms. Aloni, I'm going to throw up." Convenient, but true.

As she turns toward me, Lucus stuffs the heart in his pocket.

"I suggest you excuse yourself," she says.

I practically sprint from the room.

By the time I reach the darkened art room on the other side of the school, I'm breathing hard. I barge inside and sink down against the wall, sucking in the dusty sweetness of varnish and tempera paints.

I struggle to "get a grip," as Judith would say.

Lucas is right. It's stupid to be upset about lipstick and a poem.

But I didn't sleep last night. Instead, I thought about Sam's lips. Her voice. The way opinions seem to spill from her. The way she doesn't seem to care who's watching or listening. The way she looked at the huckleberry blossom.

Sam, Sam and Sam.

I live in a forest. You'd think there would have been things before now that I wanted but couldn't have. Lego, or video games, or store-bought cookies. But I don't remember wanting anything, ever, like I want Sam.

Except if he wanted her bad.

What the hell?

This was her attempt at apology, lipsticking my locker and writing that poem. Which proves that she doesn't know anything about me. We're two different kinds of people, and our lives are completely incompatible.

That smile, as if everything goes her way, always…

She's taken over my brain.

The door beside me swings open, and the lights flick on. I pull in my legs so Mr. Pires doesn't trip over me, but he stumbles anyway.

"You scared the hell out of me, Isaac," he says, shaking his head. "What are you doing in here?"

What *am* I doing in here?

"Hiding."

He grunts. Then he moves around me, setting up his classroom. Once the bell rings, noise swells in the hallway. Lockers open and slam.

As Mr. Pires spreads papers and black pastels on the tables, I remember the project from my own eighth-grade class. You draw a scene in pastels, then dip the paper in a color wash. It's the advanced equivalent of crayons and watercolors from kindergarten.

"What class do you have first?" he asks me.

"Lit."

He grabs one of his arriving students and sends him running upstairs with a note for the lit teacher. Then he drags an easel into one corner and chucks a paintbrush at me.

I fumble it, surprised.

"The art room's not for hiding," he says. "Start painting."

So that's what I do. To the eighth graders, I must be an extra piece of art-room furniture. They ignore me, and I ignore them. I'm in my own world, painting a post-forest-fire scene of black on black. Black clouds. Black ground. Blackened stumps and twisted wood. Then one half-hidden bloom of fireweed. Color to relieve the eye.

When I finally stand back to look at the canvas, I realize the flower's the same shade as Sam's lipstick.

Around me, kids are cleaning up their stations and getting ready for the next bell.

Mr. Pires stops beside me and tilts his head.

"Interesting," he says finally. "The magenta's a little much."

It *is* a little much. But without it, there's only the black and the gray.

"You planning to join your regular classes?" he asks.

I nod. "I'll fix this later," I say.

As soon as I figure out the answer.

•

I make it through the whole day with no further incidents. Maybe it's because I eat alone in my truck, or maybe Lucas has warned her. Sam doesn't turn up for our lunch date. I barely talk to anyone until the final bell rings. Then I push open the doors to the parking lot and find Judith leaning against my passenger side, a backpack at her feet.

"What are you doing here?"

"Got the evening off," she says. "Thought I'd hitch a ride home with you. Stay the night."

She says this casually, as if it happens often. Really, Judith's only been home twice since she left last year. This is a gift. Not so much for me, because I get to see her during the week. But for Mom and Dad, her visits are like appearances of the prodigal.

"You're going to brave the bears?"

Judith always says it's the bears that keep her away. And it's true, she's never loved them. Not even Hazel.

"The bears can mind their own business," she says, swinging herself into the truck. She's wearing tight black jeans and a top that's cut short to show her flat belly. Long silver earrings glint against her dark hair. She's about as prepared for a hike as Sam was, and my sister should know better. She should know what Dad's going to say about that shirt, too.

"You bring a sweater?"

She rolls her eyes. She's already rolled down the window and draped an arm over the edge. As we pull from the parking lot, a low wolf whistle follows us. I'm pretty sure it's not for my wheels.

"What about that guy I met at your place? Garrett. Won't he be missing you tonight?"

"He'll survive," Judith says. She reaches to flick the radio on and cranks the volume.

To be honest, I'm happy to drive her away from that guy. My sister's a smart girl. She got straight As in twelfth-grade calculus and chemistry. She can do numbers in her head that I can't do on paper. But she's not quite so smart in the life department.

Not that I have any right to judge, these days.

We pass the old grain elevators along the railway tracks at the west edge of town. The road loops past an industrial area and a few trailer parks before it reaches a patchwork of small farms. Horses stand grazing in one. Sheep in another. Then the farmland turns to marsh, and finally the south shore of the lake appears. My sister has fallen asleep beside me, her head lolling against her shoulder, mouth slightly open, one hand curled against her cheek like a little kid's.

I turn off the music and let the sound of the wind push against my ears. Let it clear out my brain.

Slowly, the highway begins to twist, blasted cliffs rising on our right and dropping sheer to the water on our left. The narrow road is like a gateway between town life and mountain. Here and there, bridges span creeks. White water foams below. Eventually, the cliff edges begin to smooth and a few scattered driveways appear. Lakeside bays or cliffside retreats. Salmo. Balfour. Kuskanook. At each driveway, a different sign. The Appleton Place, with cheery red and green apples along the edges of the board. The Rolley Retreat, on a sign made entirely of driftwood. Eagle's Aerie, words in a painted nest.

We swing past the campground and reach the overgrown entrance to the old logging road. There's no welcoming signpost here, only a yellow forestry gate to keep out visitors. Through some magic (if pot sales can be considered magical), my dad has keys to this.

I hop out of my truck, free the padlock and swing open the metal arm. When I climb back in, Judith's awake and pulling a sweatshirt from her pack.

It takes me only a moment to relock the gate once we're through. Then it's a short drive to where we stash the truck in the brush at the side of the road. Here we switch to the ATV.

"You want to drive?"

"Absolutely not," Judith says.

So I gun it a little up the trail to make her squeal and beat her fist against my shoulder. Which makes me laugh and repeat.

"Why does this trip get longer every time I come?" Judith grumbles when we ditch the four-wheeler and start hiking.

"Maybe because you're getting old?"

She swats at me.

Once we're in the trees, my lungs expand. I suppose most people relax when they open their front door and smell dinner cooking. For me, it's as I step into these hemlocks.

"Smells like home," I say. The air is thicker here, and richer, and every problem of the outside world seems a little farther away.

"Smells like trouble," Judith says.

I stop. She's below me on the trail, panting.

"You don't have to come," I say. It's true that Mom and Dad treat her like the prodigal daughter but it's also true that we all walk a tightrope when she's around.

"Don't get your panties in a knot," she says. "It'll be fine."

I take a deep breath, running a hand through my hair.

"What's with you, anyway?" she says.

When I don't answer, she takes a few giant steps to catch up to me and reaches to knead my shoulders a few times.

"You know what it means when you dream of a tepee and a wigwam?" This is classic Judith.

"What?"

"You're two tents."

When I smile instead of laugh, she says, "Two tents! Get it?"

"I get it." And now I'm laughing.

"Tell your big sis," she says once we're hiking again. "Spill it."

She's going to make a great psychiatrist one day.

I tell her. Since she already knows about Sam, it doesn't take long to explain. The locker. The poem. The smile and opinions and earlobes.

"You think you're the first person this has happened to? You can't hide in the woods forever, bro. And you've hit the transition — one foot here, one foot in the real world. It's only going to get harder until you leave."

Except that I'm not leaving.

Everyone assumes I'll do what they've done. Dad assumes I'll work on the grow. Judith assumes I'll leave. Mr. Pires assumes I'll go to art school. Sam assumes...well, who knows what that girl thinks?

But there's no way I would leave these woods for a bartending job, or psychology classes, or hot dates. Not even if those dates were with Sam.

I'm repeating this to myself so firmly and so many times that I don't immediately notice the noise. Not until Judith's feet stop moving.

At her low hiss, I lift my head, and that's when I hear it. The faraway purr of rotors.

Though I keep my feet moving, my mind shifts entirely to sound-tracking. The noise grows slowly louder, until I can distinguish the individual *thump-thump* of helicopter blades.

They'll have heard it at home by now. If Dad's working outside, he'll make sure he's sheltered by the trees. He'll stay still. Mom will adjust the camouflage netting over the vegetable garden. Inside the house, Walt will simply stop and listen, the same way I'm doing.

There's nothing else to be done. Our clearing looks the same as a dozen others on this mountain, surrounded by trees and carpeted in ferns. We leave nothing brightly colored outside. The cabin is shadowed by evergreens and half-covered by moss. It should be invisible from the air.

Thump-thump-thump.

Part of me sees the mountainside the way the helicopter pilot must see it, like a green fleece blanket flicked over granite. Deep cuts in the trees here and there, carved by creeks. Maybe a bear in the clearing, slowly picking his way between meals.

Thump-thump-thump.

As it passes overhead, Judith and I tuck ourselves against tree trunks. I crane my neck to see the colors on the side of the chopper. It's yellow and green with a bubbled front and a flat finned body, like a bottom-feeding fish that's taken to the sky.

An air crane.

They don't use them much up here, but the logging companies bring one in every once in a while. Nothing to worry about, usually, though any pilot who sees something unusual is capable of calling in a tip to the local police detachment.

Once the chopper passes, I blow out a long breath.

"I told you. This trip gets longer every time," Judith says.

I don't bother answering, and we're silent the rest of the way. Silent as we approach the clearing.

Maybe that's why it happens.

5

I hear the metallic *click-click* as he cocks his rifle. Diving sideways, I take Judith down with me. We land on the ground with a wallop. I feel the breath whoosh from her lungs as she flattens beneath me. My shoulder hits a root and scrapes along it.

A round cracks past.

"Walt, it's me! It's Isaac."

Another shot, echoing off the trees.

Crazy-ass delusional granddad shoots the pants off his grandkids. That'll make good headlines.

One more shot. This time bark splinters above me.

"Walt! Dad!" I holler.

Judith is half-buried in the leaves, arms wrapped around her skull.

"Pop! Put it down!"

It's my dad's voice, finally, and the tension flows from me as I hear him crashing toward the cabin. "It's just Isaac."

It's not just Isaac, though. It's Judith, too, slowly unwrapping her arms and turning over, her body dotted with moss and bits of rotten wood.

"What the hell?" she breathes. At least she's breathing.

"Welcome home, sis."

That's all I can think to say. I flex my shoulder back and forth, making sure it's not permanently damaged. Judith sits up and does her own inventory.

Nothing broken. Nothing shot. She's going to be bruised from head to toe, though.

I reach to pick a twig from her hair.

"This place is an asylum," she says.

Dad yells from the cabin. "You all right?"

"Be there in a minute!" I call back.

But neither of us moves toward him. Instead, I sink back against a log. My body feels shaky.

This is how Sam must have felt after her run-in with Hazel.

"And I thought I was saving you from some bad-luck guy for the night," I say.

"The woods are full of them."

I start laughing then. I can't help it. I'm not sure whether it's all laughing, or laughing with a bit of crying mixed in. Whatever it is, Judith's doing the same. Soon I have to sit like Sam was, with my head between my knees.

We're still on the ground when Dad stomps over.

"What's all this about?" he says, staring down at us.

"Maybe…trying not to get shot?"

His gaze shifts from me to Judith — as if her arrival and the gunshots might be connected — then back to me.

"Don't be a smart aleck," he says. "Helicopter must have riled him up. You should have called out as you approached."

I tell myself that he was scared, and that he doesn't mean to be so curt, and that this is how his thoughts come out under stress. But sitting beside Judith makes me hear his words the way she must hear them. No welcome. No apology for Walt, who just tried to kill us. Nothing but a shake of his head, as if he can't believe how stupid we are.

He stomps away, leaving us to pick ourselves up and brush each other off.

"Home sweet home," Judith mutters as she starts walking.

We reach the cabin just as Mom arrives, half-dripping, her hair wrapped in a towel. She must have been at the pool up the creek.

"Judith! You're here! But I heard shots…" Her eyes flick back and forth between us.

"We're fine," I tell her.

"Walt," Judith says.

Mom wraps her arms around my sister and ushers her into the cabin. Soon the two of them are chattering like chipmunks. I follow them inside and pretend to do homework while I listen. When Judith tells Mom about Garrett, she says he's an accountant. She doesn't bring up the brewery, or the fact they met at the bar.

Walt glares from his chair in the corner. When Dad comes in, he tries to say hello, but the girl talk takes up the whole cabin. He grunts and heads outside again to wash.

Hazel pokes her nose inside, her hind legs on the ground and her front legs on the stoop.

"If you get out of the way, I'll come out," I tell her.

She drops to all fours and backs up a step, allowing me to squeeze past.

I walk a little ways to the edge of the trees. Then I sit on a stump. When she settles beside me, I throw an arm around her.

"They're all nuts, you know."

Her head bobs. She shifts a little under my hand so I can scratch behind her ear.

I watch Dad tug his boots off again and close the door behind him. Through the walls I can hear the rumble of his voice and the softer sounds of Judith and Mom. Laughter. Then a string of curses from Walt, hard and sharp as bullets.

The bullets were a harsh bit of culture shock for Judith, but at least she knows these woods and this cabin. I imagine the scene the way Sam would have seen it if she'd come a couple miles farther through the bush.

What would she think of us all?

Walt's easy to explain. Deranged hippie. Something happened in the middle of his Vietnam tour, and my grandpa talked himself onto a plane and flew himself home to Oregon. He crossed the border to Canada and joined a commune west of here, in the Slocan Valley, with a big group of draft dodgers. That's where he met my grandma. But the commune didn't work out, so he and Grandma left to start their own little utopia, growing weed.

I know this much from Dad. Walt doesn't talk about any of it.

Grandma got cancer when Dad was a kid, and by the time she was diagnosed, it was too late. I guess Walt saw no reason to leave the mountains after that. No reason he couldn't raise a son in the woods. I imagine things were just as he wanted them, until his stroke.

What would Sam think of Mom and Dad? Neo-hippies, maybe. Is there such a thing? Or maybe she'd see them as criminals. Or hermits. Anarchists. Libertarians.

How many kids get shot at on the way home from school? For a brief moment, I see my family in a Jackson

Pollock splatter painting, all explosions of color. This is not the type of painting I want to create.

There's a thought pushing at me, the way Hazel pushes her head under my chin, demanding more attention. I shove it away as the cabin door swings open.

"Isaac?" Mom calls. "Dinner's ready!"

"On my way," I answer, using Hazel's flank to push myself up.

Dinner takes a bad turn halfway through. I don't know why Mom and Dad can't just enjoy the moment.

Dad starts it.

"How's work? Still at the hotel?"

"It's fine," Judith says.

"Must be busy," Mom says.

"I'm fine."

"Going to church?" Dad asks.

Judith smiles. I can see her trying to keep the conversation light. "Sometimes I sit in the orchard and have my own church. Kinda like yours," she says.

For a minute, there's only chewing. Dad's knife scrapes against his plate as he cuts through his slice of pheasant.

I can't help picturing the guy coming out of Judith's bus. They weren't praying in there.

"Fucking prick," Walt says. Hopefully his stroke hasn't given him telepathic powers.

It's enough to set Dad off.

"Don't go making excuses to yourself," he says, punctuating his words with little jabs of his fork in the air. "Before you know it, you're on the wrong road."

"Dad, I'm not on the wrong road."

"I'm just saying that living on your own can be rough. You got dreams, this psychologist thing, you work hard to make it happen. You don't sit around in the orchard pretending you're getting somewhere."

"I'm taking classes, Dad," Judith says.

"Otherwise you may as well come back here," he says.

"Fucking prick," Walt offers.

"You gotta be accomplishing — "

"Pass the potatoes, please." Mom's voice is a little shaky. When I look up, she's blinking fast.

"Now, Marion," Dad says.

"I know. I know," Mom says, forcing a smile. She reaches over and squeezes Judith toward her briefly. "I just miss her. That's all."

"I'm only telling her — "

"It's okay, Dad. I get it," Judith says.

But they've ruined it. She's already pushing back her chair and picking up her plate. And I know why. A dose of Mom guilt is just as crushing as a Dad lecture.

"Isaac, I know it's late, but you think you could give me a ride home?" Judith asks. "You can stay the night."

Goodbyes are quiet, although Mom hugs Judith so hard and so long that my sister practically has to pry herself away.

Outside, we get about three steps from the cabin before Hazel blocks the way. I can see the dark outline of Big Bugger, too, and Queenie at the edge of the trees.

"Jeez," Judith mutters. "Why doesn't Walt shoot something useful?" She tries to skirt Hazel, but the bear moves to follow.

"Isaac, can you get her away from me? I can't handle this right now."

So I give the big hairy head a push. "Stay home. I'll be back tomorrow."

Hazel settles onto her haunches with a little groan, like

a kid getting left behind. The other bears decide to keep their distance.

We stumble our way down the trail by flashlight, the route twice as long in the dark. At one point there's a strange, crackling cry above us, then the answering hoot of a mother owl from a short distance away, reassuring.

It starts to rain as we climb onto the ATV. Within minutes, we're soaked through.

"What on earth made me think I wanted to go home for a family dinner?" Judith yells into my ear, as I lean forward to pick out the rutted track in the headlights.

I have no answer.

Once she's safely tucked into the passenger seat of my truck, Judith wrings the water from her hair. I rub my hands together, waiting for the blood to return before I turn the key.

I'm down the logging road, through the gate and onto the pavement before my sister speaks again.

"Isaac, our family is certifiable."

I grunt.

"I'm serious," she says, putting a hand on my arm. "You don't see it because you've always been there, but that's not what life is supposed to be. We should be going to parties and meeting people and exploring job options."

"You're doing all those things," I say.

"Trying, at least. What about you? You can't keep living with lunatics."

And there it is — the thought that was pushing at me as I sat outside before dinner.

It's me that's crazy, not Sam. I live in the middle of a forest. On a grow-op. With bears. And I get shot at on my way home.

But this is how I've spent every single day of my life.

"I can't leave," I tell Judith.

"They're grown-ups. They *choose* to live there. You can choose something else," she says.

I can't.

But maybe I can take half a step away. A temporary emotional leave of absence. Maybe I can get to know Sam, just for this last month or so before I graduate. Maybe I can even make some real progress in my painting, before I retreat to the woods on a more permanent basis.

Would it be so unforgivable if I took a little time off, for fun?

"Promise me you'll think about it," Judith says.

All the way to town, the spin of the truck wheels on the wet pavement and the swish of the wipers sound like words. *Temporary. Absence. Temporary. Absence.*

By the time we pull into Judith's driveway, it's almost eleven.

As she unlocks her door, I can hear her cell buzzing from inside. She's left it sitting on her counter.

It stops, but starts again before we've peeled off our jackets.

Judith grabs it and has a whispered conversation with whoever's on the other end.

"Yes."

"That's okay."

"No, I understand. You didn't mean it."

"Of course."

"I can't right now."

"My brother."

"Okay, then."

Partway through the call, Judith tucks her chin and twirls her hair in her fingers. Her voice turns softer. After she puts the phone down, it rings again. She picks it up, listens, giggles and hangs up. When her eyes meet mine, she blushes.

"What?" she says.

"That your new guy?"

"I don't know if I'd call him my guy. Yet." She touches her hair again.

I know I shouldn't say it, but the words come out anyway. I'm no better than Dad, I guess.

"I didn't like the looks of him."

"You don't even know him, Isaac."

I shrug. Can't argue with that.

"Besides, you've got your own issues to deal with."

Can't argue with that, either.

"Don't be so hard on people, Isaac. We're all muddling through, you know?"

She folds down her kitchen table into a lumpy foam bed, tucks a sheet around the edges and tosses me a pillow and blanket.

"Thanks for bringing me home," she says. The boyfriend/girlfriend conversation appears closed.

"Anytime." I put a hand on her arm before she can walk away. "You know I'd do anything you needed, right?"

A sappy smile crinkles her eyes. She nods.

"I know," she says. A few minutes later, she whispers goodnight from her bunk and flicks off the light.

The darkness isn't as complete here as it is at home. Through the edges of the curtains I can see the glow of a distant porch lamp. Instead of the creek, I hear the drum of rain on the metal roof.

Am I hard on people? I like to think I'm open-minded, but maybe I'm not.

I flip over on the thin foam, punching my pillow into better shape.

Sam told her friends about Hazel, but to her, Hazel was just a bear. Most people would probably tell their friends about running into a wild animal in the woods. And it wasn't really Sam's fault she embarrassed me, either. Plenty of guys would have laughed when they found their locker decked out in lipstick. Lucas did.

In the morning, I'll explain that I'm not the kind of guy who likes the spotlight.

Then I'll get to work on my temporary leave of absence.

6

Lucas leans against his locker, absorbed in a car manual of some sort. When I get close, he looks up and smiles.

"I didn't mean to give you a hard time yesterday," he says.

"No big deal." I shove my pack into my locker.

"Bygones?" he asks.

I don't know why he's so concerned, but he appears sincere.

"Bygones," I repeat.

"Good. 'Cause I like you, man. I'd hate to think things were going to be uncomfortable." Then he holds out his fist and I follow, and he leads the sort of complicated handshake at which drug lords in movies are inherently skilled.

I am not skilled.

I do have drugs, however. They're in a paper bag that looks as if it might contain a peanut-butter sandwich. When I pass it over, he stuffs it in his pack. In return, I accept enough cash to fund a couple of fast-food meals. Ever since Judith got me hooked on fries, Mom's roasted balsamroot has never tasted quite the same.

"I have to find Sam before the bell," I tell Lucas.

Which is a stupid thing to say, because he nods knowingly.

I walk away before our newly sealed friendship gets cracked again.

It was that nod — that too-cool-for-this-life head tilt — that got me supplying Lucas in the first place.

These days, no one pays me much attention at school. I'm like an extra drinking fountain or a spare shoe under a locker. But a few years ago, it felt as if I wore bumper stickers on my forehead. Uncomfortable in Public. Misses All Pop Culture References.

Going from the backwoods to the petri dish of eighth grade was not without challenges. So when I smelled a whiff of pot on Lucas one day, I asked if he smoked. He said only when he could get his hands on weed, which wasn't nearly often enough. The next morning I turned up with our first paper bag. I guess I bought myself some insulation, though I didn't think of it that way at the time.

I can hear Sam's voice before I even open the door to the auditorium. I slip inside, wiping my palms on my jeans. While I'm hiding in the shadows between the door and the back row of seats, she's at center stage, shading her eyes with one hand, calling instructions to the person in the lighting booth. Something about blocking. She doesn't see me until I inch my way up the aisle. Then she stops, mid-sentence.

"I'll be back in a bit, okay?" she calls to the person in the booth before hopping from the stage. When she reaches me, I take her hand and pull her into the back row.

As soon as we've dropped into the seats, she starts talking.

"I embarrassed you. I'm so sorry. It's a failing of mine. I'm generally embarrassing to be around. I can only be friends with insensitive people because of it." She presses my hand earnestly while she talks.

"It's fine."

"It's not fine. I saw Lucas and he said you were uncomfortable."

I shrug. I'm not used to these torrents of words.

"I was hoping you'd come find me at lunch yesterday, Zac."

I like the way she's chosen her own name for me. One that no one else uses.

"This whole thing is twisted because my card was meant to be an apology," she says. "Now I'm apologizing for apologizing."

"You don't have to. I wanted to — "

My words will only seep, the way you can press on moss, and a few drops squish out around the edges.

But she's waiting now, biting the edge of her lip. She looks like she'll wait forever.

Get it together, I tell myself. *Spit it out.*

"I'm the one who should apologize. I overreacted."

Her smile hits at high wattage. Like someone swiveled the stage lights onto us.

"I don't like being the center of attention," I tell her.

"Listen, there are people who love it and people who avoid it. I tend to be a spotlight personality, and you're not. But opposites attract, right?"

I open my mouth to answer, but nothing comes out. Does she mean "attract" as a reference to physical attraction, or as a figure of speech? I try to find a way to ask, but maybe I've already squished all available water from the moss. Hopefully she can't see my red cheeks in the semi-darkness.

"I could make it up to you," Sam says.

"I'm not sure I can handle that." There. My words are back.

She laughs, and any remaining tension drops from my shoulders. I lean back in my seat. I think I'm smiling again.

"How about a milkshake after school? My treat."

"All right."

"All right?" She's bouncing a little on the chair.

"All right."

She kisses me. Not a romance movie, deep-throat kiss. But a kiss. On the lips. And then she's racing back up the aisle toward the stage, yelling instructions and apologies to the other people on stage, and laughing at the same time.

I stand slowly and fumble my way to the double doors.

For the rest of the day, my brain absorbs nothing. Mr. Gill asks me something, then stands over my desk and glowers.

"Are we having an epileptic episode, Mr. Mawson? A petit mal seizure?"

The class laughs on cue.

I still can't understand his question.

It's not until I'm sitting in a Burger Barn booth drinking a chocolate shake that I can reason again. And even these thoughts seem filtered through some sort of whipped-cream cloud. Sam holds my hand across the table. The edge of her foot touches mine.

I can feel people glancing toward us as they line up at the counter for their fries or their Cokes.

Then Sam starts talking about her play, and I forget to worry about the watchers.

"It's like dunking yourself in an alternate world, you know? I come out of the auditorium sometimes, and I don't know whether it's going to be light or dark outside."

"I feel like that when I'm painting," I say.

"So you get it," Sam says. "It probably sounds crazy to everyone else."

"It's not crazy. It means you're completely into it. You're not thinking about homework or sleep or what you want for dinner. You're…"

"Immersed."

Her skin is the same color as my milkshake, and perfectly smooth. When we stand up from the table, she has whipped cream on her upper lip.

I want to kiss her again. But as I'm calculating angles and deciding which foot has to step forward, she's already heading for the door, waving to friends as she goes.

Still, I might have a girlfriend, I think, after I've dropped her at her house and pointed myself toward home. My fingers tap rhythms on the steering wheel, as if I drank a dozen coffees instead of a shake.

•

At lunchtime on Friday, I knock on Judith's door. She answers wearing boxer shorts and a hoodie.

"Get dressed," I tell her. "We have to go downtown."

"Why?"

"Because I need new clothes."

I looked at my jeans this morning and couldn't remember when I'd bought them. Yesterday, when I slung an arm around Sam between classes, she wrinkled her nose.

"You smell like the woods," she said.

I dropped my arm.

"In a good way."

I'm pretty sure she was being polite.

Judith comes through as I knew she would. Within twenty minutes I'm locked in a change room at a store I've never noticed before, as my sister throws more and more "options" over the door. I try on three pairs of jeans and almost get stuck in a shirt with a zipper. A shirt which I am never, ever going to wear, no matter how bad my other clothes smell.

"Stop!" I say finally, escaping the cubicle before she can bury me entirely. "Just tell me which ones to buy."

Of course she chooses the zipper.

"Not that one."

I end up at the register with a pair of jeans, a couple of pairs of shorts and four new T-shirts.

When I asked for cash this morning, Mom gave me what seemed like an obscene amount. But fashion apparently costs money.

"Do you want to wear one of these? I could cut the tags off?" The girl behind the register is draped in an off-the-shoulder shirt with hoop earrings that almost reach her shoulders. She's looking at me with the same slight nose-wrinkle Sam wore yesterday.

"That would be perfect," Judith says.

So I find myself in the cubicle one more time.

"I'm not going back there for five more years," I tell Judith once we're safely on the sidewalk. My heart is pounding as if a helicopter just swept over.

She pats my shoulder. If I were shorter, I think she would pat my head.

"But thank you," I say.

"Anytime."

Back at school, Sam notices my new shirt immediately. In a good way.

I think I might wear this one for the rest of the week.

•

On Sundays, Dad preaches. All the words he's been holding inside his head during the week pour out in a burst of evangelic fervor, and it's as if he's talking to the entire forest rather than the three of us.

During the winter we sit around the kitchen table for his services, but when the weather improves, we troop to a nearby clearing — what Mom calls the cathedral. A fallen log provides a bench for her and Walt, and an old stump allows Dad to lean when his back gets sore.

Today I settle cross-legged in the moss, while Hazel and the twins elect to watch from the edge of the trees. I absentmindedly scratch the shape of an earlobe into the dirt, until Dad looks at me sternly, as if I'm a toddler.

"If we're ready?" he says.

He begins his first prayer. "Thank you, our Heavenly Father, for the abundance of food which you have provided for us. Thank you for friendship and kinship on this day. Thank you for good weather and good harvests to come."

"Fucking prick," Walt says.

"We pray you'll bring healing where needed, to our bodies and to our minds. We pray you'll help us focus our thoughts on the righteous..."

It's always interesting to hear one of Dad's prayers. It's like a window into his brain. I wonder if Mom, too, waits for Sundays to learn what her husband's thinking about.

We stand and sing "Awake My Soul and with the Sun." I'm not a singer, but Mom and Dad both have decent voices. Sometimes, when their notes twine together just right, I can almost see the sound rising into the canopy.

As we sit again, even Walt is quiet. Dad opens his Bible and begins his sermon.

He tells a story about three servants. Their boss goes away and entrusts them each with money. The first two invest their portions and have extra to give their boss when he returns. But the third buries his share. That guy gets tossed.

When he's finished the parable, Dad motions to the forest around us.

"All this has been given to us," he says. "We're meant to use it wisely, to cherish it and to make it grow."

He continues, and I nod every once in a while as if I'm paying close attention, but in my head I'm still with the servants. The two who invested and the one who buried. Was it really so bad for the guy to bury his gift? He kept it safe, at least. No hasty decisions or wild risks. Those other two could have lost everything.

Back at the cabin, Mom dishes us veggie soup and I take mine to the front stoop. Hazel noses up beside me. Once I've finished, I let her lick the bowl like an overgrown puppy. Then she plops down, gazing into the trees as if she's trying to see what I'm staring at.

Often there's a feeling I get after Dad's sermons. It's as if church puts everything back in balance. For a few hours, the birds sing exactly what they're supposed to sing, the trees grow just as they're supposed to grow, and I'm right where I'm supposed to be.

But today I'm still thinking about Dad's story. About

needing to make proper use of our gifts. I know that Dad thinks of this place — our cabin and these woods — as his gift.

When I think of gifts, though, I think of something different. I think of painting.

I make my way through the trees toward the drying shed, where we spread the crop every August. Though it's empty at this time of year, a pungent waft of Draft Dodger Dark greets me as I unlatch the door. Beside me, Hazel snorts.

I wait for my eyes to adjust. Slowly, charcoal patterns emerge from the walls. One wall is a crowded street scene in San Francisco — shoppers and storefronts and signs. The next wall features an old-fashioned muscle car. The third is a house with baskets of flowers hanging from the eaves.

I once asked Dad if it was Walt's house, the place he grew up, but Dad didn't know.

"It's like looking at cave paintings, isn't it?" I say now.

Hazel doesn't answer.

Walt can draw. Or he could, at least, before his stroke. He could draw better than I can. But as far as I can tell, the only art he's created in the last few decades is here in the backwoods, smelling like skunk.

This seems like the official definition of burying your gift. So is Walt the third servant? And what does that make me?

I back out of the shed and carefully relatch the door. Then I nudge Hazel's shoulder.

"Do you think Mom and Dad will understand if I'm gone a little more often this month?" I ask her.

Hazel grunts. If she has suggestions for life planning, she doesn't share them.

•

Sam is leaning against the wall again, waiting, when I pull into the school parking lot on Monday morning. She jogs toward my truck and climbs inside.

Before I realize what's about to happen, she leans across the seat and plants a kiss on my lips. As if we've been together for years. As if I'm used to having girls in my truck, or in my life at all for that matter.

I think my new shirts are working.

She shuts the door behind her.

"Let's get out of here," she says.

I glance at the school, then back toward her. She's tough to figure out, this girl. She's like two or three personalities wrapped into one. When we had milkshakes together, she said only good things about school. She told me she liked Creston so much better than her last town.

Now she wants to ditch. Now she's the girl who climbed out of her dad's car and hiked into bear territory for the heck of it.

And let's not even talk about that poem. What kind of person has the guts to write that?

Maybe women are as unpredictable as bears.

She reaches over and beeps the horn.

"C'mon. Do it, Zac. Start the truck and peel out of here."

Her grin is like a dare. My keys are back in the ignition.

The passenger door flies open. Lucas stands there, swaying slightly. He's stoned. I see it, then I smell it.

"What the heck?" I shake my head. It's not even 9:00 a.m.

Sam's already sliding into the middle of the bench seat and patting the upholstery beside her.

"Climb in," she says. "We're getting out of here."

Lucas does. He clambers up, slams the door and lets his head flop against the seat back.

I drive.

I guess my subconscious decides where we're headed. I could go west, over the summit. I could drive east on the long straight highway that leads to Cranbrook, a slightly larger and grittier version of Creston.

But I head north, toward home.

Or rather, toward the campground.

Lucas explores the webbing between his fingers in the glow of the sunlight.

Sam and I glance at each other. I give a small shrug. Just because our lockers are together doesn't mean I understand the guy.

"Rough morning?" I ask.

"Family issues?" Sam asks at the same time. She's braver than I am.

I take my eyes off the highway for long enough to see Lucas nod. It's hard to tell if it's really a nod, or if his head is too heavy for his neck.

"Anything we can do?" Sam asks.

"I've got it covered," he says. He raises one finger, as if he's a professor about to lecture. Then he gets distracted by a hangnail.

"There's a lot of...pressure," he says eventually. "I generally think of myself as an expert in handling pressure. But sometimes...this morning, for example...it grows more crushing, and I find myself needing a pressure release. A valve." He really does sound like a professor. Except stoned.

Sam smiles the same crooked smile that got me on the hiking trail in the first place.

"We understand exactly," she says.

I glance at her again, wondering what made her need to skip school this morning. And I think about Lucas's word.

Crushing. I don't feel crushed, exactly. I feel like opposing forces are pulling at me.

Sam's fingers are resting lightly on my thigh, which is causing a different sort of pulling.

"So…your parents?" Sam asks Lucas.

He shrugs. "My dad feels very strongly about a certain type of achievement."

Something doesn't make sense to me. "Isn't your dad a…"

"Psychologist."

Sam laughs.

"I know. It's a classic case." Lucas turns to Sam, finger raised again. "I have a rationalization. I know that my father's father was a man prone to violence. Are you following me?"

We're following him.

"It is my personal belief that Dad became a psychologist to determine where things went wrong."

"But…" I don't want to say the obvious.

"Well, he's trying. He doesn't always succeed, that's all."

When we don't answer, he turns his head toward Sam a little.

"What profession does your father pursue?"

"He's a member."

"He's RCMP?" Lucas asks.

"Yeah."

I almost drive off the road. Lucas puts a hand on the dash to steady himself. Sam's fingernails imprint my leg.

"Sorry. Thought I saw a deer." I force my hands to unclench a little on the steering wheel.

RCMP. A cop.

I may not know exactly which path I'm supposed to be on, what I'm supposed to be burying and what I'm supposed to be investing, but this is not a good development. I'm in my truck with the daughter of a cop, on my way to the campground nearest my family's grow-op.

I think I've screwed up.

7

It's hard to drive with my thoughts spinning around like cop car cherry lights, but I manage to get us to the campground. I circle past the first loop of gravel sites, then pull to the side of the dirt road and take a deep breath of the quiet.

Each tent pad here is a perfect square. The sun has finally crested the mountains and steam rises from a canvas tent here and there. An older couple sips coffee near a small RV. The lake glistens through the trees from across the highway.

Lucas has gone silent, eyes closed, but Sam looks around curiously.

"You have a plan?" she asks.

I'm embarrassed, suddenly.

"I thought we might visit someone. A guy who may or may not be living in a treehouse." It's not exactly a plan. It's simply what I've wanted to do ever since I heard Mom and Dad talking about him.

I manage to explain to Sam what my mom said about the druid who stayed behind after the convention.

"The thing my dad checked on that day," she says.

"Right. Because your dad's a..." My words trail off, but Sam doesn't seem to notice.

"And this guy lives up a tree," Lucas says, his eyes open again. Well, one eye, at least.

"Up a tree," I confirm.

"Impressive."

"It *is* a little awesome," Sam says.

I know where the old treehouse is. This is practically my backyard, after all. I doubt there's a place on this whole mountain that Judith and I haven't climbed on or up or into. One dry summer we even climbed through the culvert that shuttles the creek beneath the highway. So we've been to the treehouse, though I can't imagine living there. As I remember, it was a few rotting boards dripping with moss.

I lead Sam and Lucas up the hill above the tent sites, picking through the underbrush and holding back branches for them. It doesn't take long to reach the platform.

He's made a few improvements.

Modern druids have the advantage of nylon. He's stretched an orange tarp in the canopy, one corner tied lower, with a pail dangling underneath to catch the rain. Looking more closely, I can see he's used a combination of rope and driftwood to reinforce the floor. He's even lashed a railing around the edge. The bottom of a red sleeping bag dangles from one side.

"Swiss Family Robinson," Lucas says, staring upward.

"Hello?" Sam hollers.

Though there's clearly no one on the platform, I somehow expect the druid to float down from the trees. I'm a little disappointed when he saunters from the brush.

"Welcome," he says, as if this were his backyard instead of mine. He's bushy haired and bearded, but wearing more Gore-Tex than I would have expected. No robe.

"Welcome, yourself," I say.

Sam is more friendly. "Nice place," she says. "Very unique."

"I would invite you up, but I am not sure it can hold all of us," he says. "Can I make you some tea instead?"

"Don't take tea from strange druids. I think there's a rule about that," I whisper as we trail after him.

Sam grins and elbows me.

The druid's name is Amir and he's originally from Iran. An Iranian druid. Lucas laughs when he hears this, then unsuccessfully tries turning the sound into a cough. He's still having trouble keeping a straight face when Amir leads us to an old VW Van.

There are lawn chairs. Druid life is not what I imagined it would be.

Within a few minutes, we're sipping mint tea from travel mugs. Amir lights a joint and passes it to Sam and Lucas, who suck in a lungful each. I wave it away. I don't usually smoke. For all his pride in Draft Dodger Dark, Dad has strong ideas about the effects of pot on the teenage brain.

"So, I don't get it," Sam says after a while, turning to Amir. "You have a van, but you're sleeping up a tree?"

Lucas can't hold it in any longer. He starts giggling like a little girl. Apparently the professor act is over.

"For the experience," Amir says. "To really *be* with myself in the forest, you understand?"

His pot is a crappy sativa hybrid, left too long on the plant. I can tell by the fumes. He could find himself more quickly if his product weren't all smoke and no substance.

I'm fairly disappointed. Maybe I was expecting an oracle. Someone with the wisdom of the woods. This guy doesn't even have the wisdom of ganja.

Sam, though, is still interested. She looks at him like a wide-eyed news reporter.

"What have you learned so far?" she asks.

"It is not about happiness," he tells her. "It is something deeper than that. A peace with who I am and where I am." There's a long pause while he inhales, holds, then slowly streams smoke from his nostrils. "Where I am in the universe, you understand?"

I can hear Walt's voice in my head. If he were here, pre-stroke, he'd have both hands on a rifle barrel by now, and he'd growl, "I'll tell you where you are in the universe, son. You're in a load of shit." He'd scare the guy right out of the woods. It would be for Amir's own good, too. Even if he doesn't fall out of his tree and crack his skull, he's going to crap his pants once Dad gets around to tossing bear dinners under his tree in the middle of the night.

If I convince this druid to leave now, it will be easier for everyone.

But I can't do it. Sam has asked him another question. In answer, he stands, plants his feet wide and opens his arms to the sky as if he's embracing the world. It's ridiculous, and yet so sincere that I can't help envying him a little. He doesn't know a thing about where he is in the universe. If he did, he'd be up the mountain dipping into pot that's a hundred times better than his. But maybe it doesn't matter. Maybe he really is finding himself. He's a guy who can embrace life in public without embarrassment. There's something to admire in that.

I get the feeling Amir doesn't feel a lot of pressure. Not out here, anyway.

Lucas hasn't managed to free himself quite so effectively.

"I gotta get back," he tells me, still shaking his head at the druid. "Math test after lunch."

Sam, too, turns to go. But I sidle a little closer to Amir.

"I should tell you, there's a ton of bears around here. You might run into one, or hear one in the night. Stay calm, okay? Most of them are harmless if you keep out of their way."

"Thank you. There is no need to worry about me. Animal spirits are part of the universe. We see each other, you understand?"

It seems Dad's usual strategies aren't going to work.

•

The three of us head back to school for the afternoon. When I pass Lucas between classes, he plants his feet in the center of the hallway and opens his arms to the universe. When I pass Sam two seconds later, she half shuts her eyes and waves one finger in the air.

Nut jobs.

I drive Sam home after school, then walk her up the driveway to her white-on-beige home, the opposite of a druid treehouse or a cabin in the woods. This entire street is perfectly squared and clipped.

"Want to come in for a while?" she asks.

She has the fingers of one hand tucked into the waistband of my jeans, and I've lost all blood flow to my brain.

Inside, it looks less like the den of a right-wing, badge-carrying powermonger than I expect. I can't even see any

Mountie memorabilia. Just a brown leather sofa facing a flat-screen TV in an open-concept living/dining room. Built-in shelves on either side of the TV display small stacks of hardcover books (mysteries and Michael Crichton), plus a few pottery bowls. There are family photos.

In one picture Sam sits between a buff, broad-shouldered Asian man and a petite blonde woman. They're nestled close on a driftwood log, leaning their heads toward one another.

It's a different Sam than the one I know. This photo version has long glossy hair, one side tucked behind her ear. She's wearing a cute purple sweater and an open smile, like nothing bad has ever happened in her world.

Sam — the evolved Sam with dark eyeliner and a skull pendant — joins me by the shelves. She sighs when she sees the photo.

"Past era," she says.

"When was it taken?"

She's already turning away, fingers scrunching the spikes on her head into confused perfection. "Couple of summers ago. Want to see better pictures?"

Which is how I end up cross-legged on her living-room carpet, flipping through an oversized scrapbook. Each page is covered with theater programs and photos from her old high school.

Sam's had parts in *Little Shop of Horrors*, *The Lottery* and *Footloose.*

As I turn the pages, she tells stories about forgotten props, last-minute improvs and performer meltdowns.

Tucked into the back of the scrapbook are theater-school brochures, which Sam reaches to straighten.

"You must have an art-school collection like this," she says.

Suddenly I feel as if I've wandered into the guidance counselor's office. I close the book.

"When do your parents get home?"

"It's just my dad, and he's working," she says. "He won't be here until after dinner."

I reach an arm around her waist.

Judith stole a bottle of old Scotch from the bar one night and we drank it together in the orchard. Kissing Sam is like shooting that Scotch. Heat flows from my lips, through my throat, all the way down my spine. My hands move along her skin without asking my brain's permission. I breathe in the smell of her, outdoor air and shampoo and cinnamon gum.

Beneath her shirt my fingers fumble. She takes pity on me, finally, and unfastens her own bra. Her skin feels like the undersides of leaves.

Her hands trail down my back, making scorch marks through my shirt.

When she pulls away, I'm breathing hard. I have to dig my fingers into my palms to keep from reaching for her again.

Then she tilts her head toward the sliding glass door and I spot something on the back deck.

"You have a hot tub."

She raises an eyebrow at me. "Want to try it?"

So that's how I end up eating crinkly Korean shrimp crackers in a hot tub with Sam, while wearing only my boxer shorts. Sam has changed into a blue bikini. The tub is completely hidden by the shrubs on one side of the yard and by the deck fencing on the other. It's as if we're in our own private pond.

For a while, we talk. About Lucas. About Sam's dad and

how he has no interest in Sam's life. She's already signed up for a week of a drama camp in Cranbrook this summer. She's applying next year to theater schools, but her dad doesn't know that part. He's never asked, apparently.

"We had dinner together last night, and for more than seven minutes, the only sound was his knife scraping against his plate," she says. "I timed it."

"What broke the silence?"

"He got a call from work."

I want to know more. I want to know what she eats for breakfast and whether she sleeps on her right side or her left. I want to know what she doodles on the edges of her notebooks. But she wants to ask things, too. When she brings up my family, I talk about Judith and her job at the bar and her bus in the orchard. I promise to take Sam there one day.

And then, because I can't answer anything else — and also for other better reasons — I put my hand on her ribcage again, and my mouth on the curve where her shoulder meets her neck.

She slides a leg across my lap. I feel lightheaded with the heat.

"This could be dangerous," I say, letting my head rest of the edge of the tub.

"You have no idea."

The way she says it makes me lift my head, look at her more closely.

"Never mind," she says.

It's easy to let her words slide, the same way my hands slide up and hers slide down. My pulse pounds in my ears.

Then I feel Sam's body tense. When I open my eyes, she's staring over my shoulder.

A deep throat clear.

I wonder frantically if I can avoid turning around, forever. But of course I turn, and meet the eyes of a fully uniformed man with a sharp-edged brush cut, an intense glare and a deep furrow in his forehead.

Sam says nothing. Not, "Dad, this guy sucking my face, his name's Isaac." Not, "You're home early." Not, "This isn't as bad as it looks."

Which would normally leave me to stand and walk across the planks of the deck and reach to shake his hand, except…I'm wearing only boxers and Sam's hand has been *right there.* It's definitely not safe to stand up yet.

I raise my fingers in a lame wave. "I'm Isaac."

"Corporal Ko."

That does it. Below the waterline, everything shrivels.

"Nice to meet you," I croak, but Corporal Ko has already turned to go inside.

"Time to wrap it up," he calls back.

I would like to wrap it up. I'd like to wrap myself in a towel and sprint for the door.

Sam, though, appears to think the entire scene is hilarious.

"You should see your face right now," she says.

I press my palms to my temples. "Is this what you meant by dangerous? When you said that I had no idea?"

"No!" she insists. "When I said that, I was talking about my mom. My parents had a raging New Year's Eve party a couple of years ago. My dad fell asleep on the couch once most of the guests had gone. When he woke up, the house was quiet, but he couldn't find Mom."

"Where was she?"

"Outside in the hot tub with another guy. Someone who worked with Dad."

I wince.

"He didn't tell me that story, of course. One of the wives told me. And all of this was in Kelowna, not here. Different hot tub."

I consider drowning myself. I'm in the hot tub of a cop, with his daughter, in the same place he once found his wife.

Personal vendetta. Revenge. Death.

I suck in a long breath while I look at Sam. She's swirling the hot tub bubbles between her palms. Her cheeks are flushed with the steam, and her hair stands in small damp spikes around her face.

I grab a towel from the edge and wrap it firmly around my waist. We're the Montagues and the Capulets and she doesn't know it.

We're everything I've been taught to avoid, my entire life.

She has no idea.

"I have to go."

There's no sign of Corporal Ko when I walk through his house a few minutes later, dressed again and holding my sopping boxers in a plastic grocery bag.

At the front door, Sam smiles up at me. "See you tomorrow."

She doesn't seem the least bit concerned.

"Sure," I say. But I duck her kiss, and I have to resist the urge to sprint to my truck.

All the way up the highway, my face burns. My insides flip and churn with the horrifying awkwardness of being caught in the hot tub with Corporal Ko's daughter and not being able to stand.

I hit the horn, the blast echoing from the rocks and making me feel, somehow, a tiny bit better.

•

I can still smell the chlorine on my skin as I hike home. Mom smells it, too.

"Did you go swimming?" she says after she hugs me. She's in the garden, picking lettuce for dinner.

"Yeah. After school with some friends."

It feels as though there are pebbles stuck in my throat. I'm not used to lying to her.

"It was a spur-of-the-moment thing," I say. I thought I had my face under control, but I flush as soon as I think about the hot tub.

I need to stop talking, because she believes me. She's turned back to her vegetables.

The days are long here this time of year. The sun is still hovering over the mountains across the lake, and Mom's garden patch looks like an Impressionist's version of green.

"I could take over here. Give you a break?" I offer.

I could spend the rest of my life weeding and never see a hot tub again.

My cheeks burn.

Don't think of hot tubs.

Mom still doesn't notice. She sends me to check on Dad.

"He's over by the clearing, I think. He's the one who might need a break."

So Hazel and I pick our way through the bracken and toward the plants, which have been growing like crazy. They're almost as big as their sword-fern partners now, and they stand out a bit against the darker green around them.

This clearing is the whole reason we live where we do. It's on a gradual slope, with perfect southern exposure.

There's the creek along the edge for water, and a steep drop a few minutes farther south to discourage any random hikers.

I spot Dad by the creek. He's diverted water into our old metal barrel, and he's hauling a bag of fertilizer toward it in a way that's guaranteed to mess with his back.

"Dad! I got it."

He drops it with a grunt and backs up a few steps.

"Is this an extra shot?"

We fertilized the plants a few weeks ago. Usually we fertilize more often when they're small and setting their leaves, then ease off as the season progresses.

"Trying to give 'em a jump," Dad says. "In case we want to harvest early this year."

I don't know why we'd need to harvest early, but I don't bother arguing. I haul the bag to chest height and dump the crystals into the barrel. The water turns a bright, impossible blue — the color of the ocean in travel-agency posters for tropical vacations. Maybe it will impart an extra vacation feel to the high. Maybe I can pretend I'm in Mexico, far away from any hot...

Once I've given the stuff a good stir, I scoop out a bucket and begin dousing the first few burlap-wrapped plants.

"You can head inside if you want," I tell Dad. "I got this."

He gives my shoulder a slap on the way past.

"Couldn't do without ya," he says.

I sigh. Ever since I met Sam's dad, I've been desperate to get home, as if I could hide in these trees and leave every embarrassing moment behind. But as soon as Dad says those words, *Couldn't do without ya*, I feel trapped.

At the edge of the clearing, Dad and Hazel become silhouettes against the trees, their figures dominating the foreground while evergreens fill the middle. A couple of puffy pink-tinged clouds rest on the blue background. Maybe I'd paint a few cannabis leaves peeking from along the edge.

I fill another bucket. And another.

Couldn't do without ya. I hear Dad's words all through dinner, dishes and homework.

I'm still hearing them as I fall asleep.

8

As I turn onto Canyon Street, the town looks like an ant colony beginning to stir. Cars nose onto the road, and a few people hurry along the sidewalk. Dad has sent me with papers to deliver, so I turn down the street by the lawyer's office — Higgens and Brown. Though I'm early, the door swings wide when I push on it.

"Hello?"

An empty reception desk.

"Hello?" I peer around the corner toward Mr. Higgens' office. He's a white-haired pot-bellied guy who seems to be wearing the same gray suit every time I see him. He's on the phone, but he waves me in. I hold up the envelope, drop it on his desk and make my escape.

Soon this sort of thing could be my only interaction with the outside world. I could operate in sign language.

The idea whines and buzzes in my head like a mosquito I can't swat.

At school, Sam is waiting beside the doors. Usually when she throws her arms around my neck or plants a kiss on my lips in the middle of the hallway, I feel as if everyone is turning to stare at us. But today I feel a rush of relief.

Before I can speak, she's telling me her latest drama news. Her interpretation of a scene last week differed from that of the teacher, apparently, and Sam is so convinced her way is right, she's going to perform it again for her today.

I interrupt. "What did your dad say yesterday?"

She scowls. "Nothing."

"Nothing?"

"It'll take more than that," she says.

To what? Have Corporal Ko plot my demise?

The bell rings before I can force Sam to clarify.

"I have drama. Gotta go." She stands on tiptoes to kiss me, then hurries down the hall. I don't see her again until lunchtime, when we climb into my truck and drive to the viewpoint along the highway, eating our sandwiches curled against one another on the bench seat.

"So...your dad really wasn't mad?" I'm finding this hard to believe.

"He doesn't care, okay? It's not a big deal."

If he didn't care, why interrupt us in the first place?

But I can tell I'm not going to get more answers. Sam's jaw is set, and she's folded her arms across her chest.

"Sometimes I can't wait to get out of here," she says finally, looking out over the fields to the mountain pass. "One day you'll see me in the ads for a big new Broadway play. And I'll see ads for your next gallery show."

I snort. "Not likely."

"Of course it's likely! Your sketches are amazing. Face it. We're both going to be ridiculously famous."

"I only paint for myself. To see what I think." In my drying shed.

Sam rolls her eyes and shakes her head as if I'm spouting nonsense.

"Whatever school you end up at, check out the performing arts options for me, okay?"

"I'm not going to school. I'm going to stick around."

She pushes herself upright so she can better eyeball me. "What are you talking about?"

I shrug.

"Don't you want to get out of here? Don't you want to have great teachers, and see galleries in other cities, and paint with other people who love painting?"

I shrug again. Of course I'd love those things. But I can't take a four-year vacation from my life just to paint, can I? That would no longer count as a temporary leave of absence.

"Well?" Sam asks.

"It's not so easy."

"It *is* easy. It's called making plans."

"I *plan* on going to English this afternoon, followed by art." I pull myself upright and put the key in the ignition.

"We're not done talking about this, Zac Mawson." Sam pokes a finger at my chest. And in that moment, it's like she knows exactly who she's supposed to be, the way my dad knows he's meant to grow pot, or Big Bugger knows he was born to rule the clearing.

•

I'm still feeling off balance by the time my art class rolls around. And Mr. Pires' latest assignment doesn't help. We're supposed to make a collage of life's important symbols, then cover it in cellophane, which will force us to draw the crinkling of light and the slight distortions that the plastic creates.

Under my cellophane, I have a tube of lipstick, donated by Sam. I've added a scrap of bright green fabric to represent Lucas's jacket. Ever since our trip to the druid, something's shifted between us. We're no longer alphabetical acquaintances, but actual friends. So there's green in my collage.

Then there's a bunch of paintbrushes fanned below the plastic, the tip of each one dipped in a different color. Cyan, vermilion, umber. I've added a lichen-mottled branch, a tree mushroom, a fern tip and a silver key like the one for my truck.

The sketching part of the assignment is going well for me. I can see the lines and shadows that make the cellophane transparent yet visible. I can draw the straight or blurred edges of the objects underneath.

But my symbols make no sense. They're the collection of someone with multiple personalities. They're objective proof of the clash between my life at home and life at school. I've been cruising along as if I can keep juggling both, but school's ending in a few weeks.

When I tear my work in half and crush the paper into the recycling bin, Mr. Pires glances up from behind his own easel. The kids around me stop moving their pencils. They don't say anything, though, as I rearrange my things and begin a new sketch.

I don't look left or right at any of them until the bell rings. Then, as they pack up, I shred my second attempt. Destroying it is somewhat satisfying.

Once the room has emptied, I corner Mr. Pires.

On his easel, there's a half-finished abstract in rich greens and blues. It's impressive enough to distract me.

"Are you giving yourself assignments, too?"

"Actually, I have a show. A gallery show in Vancouver next month. Part of a summer exhibit."

I'm surprised into momentary silence. I somehow thought Mr. Pires existed only for the education of his students. The idea of him showing his own art seems like cheating, somehow.

"Teaching isn't enough for you?"

He folds his arms and leans back against the counter.

"They're two sides of the same thing," he says eventually. "Teaching and exhibiting are both about sharing my viewpoints."

"Your views about art."

"My views about the world."

I look at his canvas again. It makes me feel as if I've jumped from a cliff into the deepest lake water. It's the exact opposite of the murals inside our drying shed. There, everything's hidden. Those are gray charcoal lines in the semi-darkness, and the only people who will ever see them are Mom, Dad and me. No one will ever walk around to view them from different angles, or talk about them with their friends, or think about their possible interpretations.

This painting of Mr. Pires, it grabs your eye. Invites everyone to look.

I glance back at my own heap of crumpled paper at the top of the recycling bin.

"I want to do a portfolio after all," I blurt.

Mr. Pires throws his hands in the air.

"Now?" he says.

For several months last fall, he and the school counselor tried to convince me to apply to art school. Unsuccessfully.

"The deadlines have passed," he says.

"But I'll have it, if I want it in the future."

Suddenly, I need to have it. I need a collection of work that I've created, so that I can know I was once a painter.

When Mr. Pires nods, a wave of relief washes over me.

"You've done some good pieces this year, Isaac. Let's have a look at them, and we'll see what we can build on."

I think of the canvases I've finished, all of them rolled and stored in plastic tubs under Judith's bus. It felt too weird to take them home.

"Your timing could be better, but I'm glad you're going to do it," Mr. Pires says. "Art school will expose you to all sorts of concepts and techniques we haven't had time to explore in class."

That's too much to think about right now. I just want my paintings photographed and collected into something real.

"It's possible to become an artist in isolation. But it's not easy," Mr. Pires says. "You'll find that society conspires to tie you to an ordinary life."

I'm not even part of society, and it's already conspiring against me. Though not in ordinary ways. Art school isn't going to happen for me. It's not even a financial possibility. Though the grow must make some cash, I've never seen much of it.

But even while I'm thinking these things, Mr. Pires is talking about landscape art and life-painting classes. I'm imagining studios full of sunlight and talent.

My temporary emotional leave of absence is extending.

"So, we'll work on a portfolio, and maybe next year you'll be ready to apply," Mr. Pires says.

Late nights in coffee shops listening to jazz musicians. Teachers who have been to New York and Paris. Museums and galleries.

I nod.

"Bring in the pieces you have at home, and we'll look through them together," he says.

More nodding.

Somewhere deep inside me, there are alarm bells and sirens. Roaring helicopter blades. But here, in the art compartment of my brain, I'm already sorting through my canvases, deciding which to choose.

•

I want to tell someone about this new plan, and I pull into the bar parking lot on my way home, knowing Judith's shift is starting.

I'm about to climb out of the truck when I spot her. She's in the alley beside the building, with Garrett standing a breath too close. I see his hand close around the bird bones of her wrist.

That's it. Just his hand. But I don't like it.

"Judith!" I call her name as I approach.

Garrett drops his hand.

"You just get done school?" he says.

"Yeah."

"Must be almost graduation time." He shows too many teeth when he grins.

"Well," he says, turning to Judith, "we should get you to work. I'll come inside and we can talk."

Translation: we can talk where your little brother can't follow.

"Actually, Judith, I need a few minutes." I give my own fake smile to Garrett. "Family stuff."

He raises his hands in mock defeat. "I get it. Who am I to stand between a woman and her family?" He makes two little guns with his fingers and takes a smarmy one-two shot at Judith. "I'll catch you later."

I don't consider myself a violent person. But the urge to punch this guy is almost irresistible. I find myself gritting my teeth as I watch him walk away.

"I'm late, Isaac," Judith says. "What do you need?"

What *do* I need? I was going to tell her about my portfolio, but now I'm not so sure. She'll jump to conclusions, for one thing. Also, it's hard to think about art when I can still smell Garrett, mixed with overripe dumpster fumes.

My sister gives him a little wave as he drives away.

"You know what? It'll wait. You get to work," I say.

"You interrupted me for no reason?"

"I'll make it up to you."

I wait until she's inside before I start the truck again. Then I head home, fantasizing about ways to get rid of Garrett more permanently. I'd love to see him meet Walt one day...

•

The makers of water pumps don't consider the challenges of mountain run-off. Every year, the filter in our pump gets clogged with mud and leaves and disgusting worm-like creatures. I'm in charge of dismantling the box, cleaning it and piecing it back together. I have to stand in the creek to detach the hoses, and even this close to summer, the water's cold enough to turn my hands purple.

Jobs like this used to be better when there were two of us.

When I cleaned the pump last spring, Judith was still living on the grow. As I stood ankle-deep in water, she watched from the bank.

"I've signed up for a bartender's course," she said.

"Need a taste-tester?"

"The hotel's even going to pay for it. My boss says he considers it an investment." She was already waitressing there on weekends.

I stopped sloshing and peered at her. "What exactly is he investing in?"

"My skills, idiot!" she said, leaning down to scoop a small tsunami toward me. "Get your head out of the gutter. I'm trying to tell you something serious."

"You want to be a bartender?" I knew that wasn't it. I was only delaying the announcement.

"Not forever." She lowered her voice. "I want to get out of here. I'm going to rent a room for a while, then get my own place. I can work for a few years and save for school."

Maybe between other siblings this would have been normal conversation. For us it felt more like treason. Judith had to stop and take a deep breath before she even said it.

"I'm going to live in town."

I let out a long slow whistle.

It isn't that Dad is opposed to town, as a concept. When we were kids, the whole family would go a couple of times a year. Dad would head to the machine shop or the farm supply. He'd drop Mom at Creston's mini-department store on the way, so she could stock up on cotton socks and boxer shorts and quilted plaid shirts.

That was town.

Dad can't believe anyone would want to live there. He found his God in the wilderness, and he can't imagine Him living anywhere else.

Judith collapsed on the creek bank to watch me work.

"I can't stay here, Isaac," she said, a note of pleading in her voice.

It wasn't me she had to convince, though I'd miss her.

"Is it because of the bears?"

"I just need my own space for a while."

At the creek that afternoon, I assumed she was still in the planning stages. I thought I'd have a few weeks to turn her ideas over in my head, like creek-tumbled stones, checking them for rough edges.

But Judith didn't give me time for that. Even before we talked, she'd already packed her things. She broke the news to Mom and Dad at dinner that night, in what turned out to be a short but loud conversation. Then she set off by herself down the trail.

Dad went after her the next day and got her set up in the bus. Maybe gave her some money, even. But that doesn't mean he agreed with her. He barely spoke for days after she left.

I finish mucking out the filter, finally. As I'm fitting it back into place, my most recent picture of Judith flashes in my head. Garrett's hand wrapped around her wrist.

I sink the hoses back into the creek with a little more force than necessary. Then I step onto the bank and take a deep breath.

I know what I'd do if I were Dad. I'd drag a few carcasses under Garrett's tree and leave him to the bears.

9

I wake at dawn on Friday to the sound of helicopter blades. Instantly I'm alert, my heart racing. I react to helicopters like other people must react to fire alarms.

I track the sound until it passes overhead, going north. Then I pull myself from the covers, shivering in the morning chill. I duck from the lean-to into the kitchen, where Dad's got coffee brewing.

"Logging chopper?"

He grunts. I can't tell if it's agreement or worry.

"Seen anything unusual lately?" he asks. I guess that means worry.

Walt sits on the edge of his bed at the side of the room, cursing. He's wearing pajama pants with a slit in the front and his junk's escaped. Dangling like wrinkled fruit.

"Depends what you mean by unusual," I say.

Dad's eyes snap up. Then he sees where I'm looking and grunts again.

"I talked to the druid." I cross the room to help Walt while averting my eyes at the same time. "The one in the campground."

Any efforts Dad has made have been unsuccessful. Amir is still on his "journey."

"Fucking prick," Walt mutters. He's halfway up now, one arm still on the cot for support. I haul him upright. Getting him ready for the day is a process sometimes.

"He seemed harmless," I say. "He's looking for his place in the universe."

"Well, it's not here. Did you tell him that?"

Walt saves me from answering. "Fucking universe." Then he demands, "Did you hear that chopper? Where the hell's my rifle?"

We're so used to ignoring Walt that it's a shock when he spits out full sentences.

Dad moves quickly to distract him. Walt's soon sitting at the table with a coffee and a couple of fried eggs in front of him. Mom hid the ammunition after he shot at Judith and me, but there's no sense taking chances.

"Keep your eyes open," Dad tells me. I assume he's referring to the choppers, not the druid. The police may have downscaled their war on drugs, but we're still technically illegal up here, especially since we're growing on land that's not our own.

I know the signs to watch for. We might spot surveillance cars at the logging road entrance as the police track anyone who accesses the property. We might see footprints on the trail. There might even be cameras. Dad's not sure if that possibility is real or rumored. They'd have to be pretty serious to start tying cameras to trees.

Dad knows people whose grow was busted. He says they had no warning. A chopper appeared overhead and police officers rappelled down to the crop. It was a specially funded program that summer, apparently. Choppers equipped with infrared. Customs officers and police working together. That was all before pot became more acceptable, but still…

I scoop a fried egg onto a piece of toast and shove it in my mouth on the way out the door.

"I'll take a look around before I head to town."

Dad nods. He stares into his coffee cup like it might be a crystal ball.

Outside, Big Bugger is sauntering away from a still-steaming shit pile. Right beside our steps.

"You did that on purpose."

He doesn't turn at my voice. Just waddles his big ass toward the clearing, as if he's king of the mountain.

"King of shit," I mutter, as I grab the shovel from the side of the cabin. I have to scrub my hands in the creek afterward, in case the smell clings to me.

I don't check the bottom of the trail for footprints. Big Bugger distracted me and I don't remember until I'm turning onto the lake road, and then it seems too late to drive back.

What I'd like to do is forget the grow for a little while. It's a teacher-development day, and I'm supposed to pick up Sam and Lucas this morning.

"Can I help you?"

At Sam's front door, I find myself face to face with her dad, who looks even more intimidating with a shadow of stubble. Sam skids to a stop behind him.

"I'm Isaac. We met once…before." I manage to stick out my hand, which he ignores.

"I'm taking Sam for breakfast?" It turns into a question because I'm on one side of him and Sam's on the other.

Sam tries to duck beneath his elbow. "Bye, Dad!"

"Wait just a minute." He grabs her arm, draws her back inside and closes the door in my face.

I shift from foot to foot on the stoop, not sure if this is the end of our breakfast plans. From inside, I can hear the low rumble of his voice and the increasingly loud pitch of hers.

Finally, Sam flings open the door and grabs my hand.

"C'mon," she says. "We're going."

I don't wait around to see whether her dad agrees.

"What did he say?" I ask, once we're a few blocks away.

Sam grins. "He called you a shitrat."

"A shitrat!" I don't know what a shitrat is, exactly, but I'm offended.

She leans over to nuzzle my neck.

"What did you want him to say? That you're a sizzling hot stud?"

"That would be uncomfortable." But then, the entire situation is uncomfortable.

It doesn't take us long to pick up Lucas and order brunch at the Bigfoot Bistro. Inside, the wood-paneled walls are papered with fifty years of newspaper reports about sasquatch sightings in the woods.

I wonder how many of those sightings can be attributed to Dad, Walt or Big Bugger.

"What are you thinking about, Zac?" Sam nudges me.

"Power-hungry dads."

Sam looks like she's going to prod further, but breakfast arrives. Across from me, Lucas devours a heaping plate of eggs and bacon. Sam sits beside me cutting her French toast and strawberries into perfect square-shaped bites.

Beneath the table, her leg presses against mine. Every

once in a while she drops a hand to my leg, and her fingernails trace patterns on my inner thigh.

I have no idea what I eat.

Soon we pile into the truck again and drive to the river, where we lie on our backs on the gravel bank like digesting anacondas. Lucas is wearing his green jacket, which adds to the effect. When I tell him he looks like a giant snake, Sam giggles.

"I love this jacket," Lucas protests.

Sam laughs harder. "You're like Mr. Squeaky Clean," she says. "Like a guy cheerleader."

"All part of my plan." Lucas grins.

The sun climbs high enough to sparkle off the water. After a while, a gang of younger kids tumbles out of the trees. It takes them only seconds to strip to their bathing suits and grab the knotted rope tied to one of the overhanging branches. The first one swings in a wide, whooping arc before plunging into the river. A few more follow, hollering their lungs out.

"I don't want a Mr. Squeaky Clean disguise," Sam says suddenly. "I'd be happier if people actually saw me. I'd rather my dad yelled or hit the wall or locked me in a tower, but he just stares at me like I'm a train wreck about to happen."

"You're not a train wreck," I whisper into the nape of her neck.

"You're not a train wreck," Lucas echoes. He's sprawled on the other side of her.

"You know what's weird? It makes me want to be a train wreck. When he looks at me like that, I feel like I may as well prove him right. Or shock him with something even worse."

"He's probably still hurt," I say. "Because of your mom."

"Of course it's because of my mom. Or my mom left because of his crap attitude."

"Why does it even matter?" Lucas asks. "One day your name's going to be on a big theater marquee and he'll know he was wrong."

Sam snorts softly.

I could trump both their family situations with mine. I know Lucas feels pressure from his parents, no matter how casual he sounds about his Mr. Squeaky plan. I know Sam is in some sort of constant Cold War with her dad. But if I told them about the grow, about how much my family needs me there and what my life will look like, forever, I could win the pressure war.

I say nothing.

After a minute, Sam stands.

"Time to go?" Lucas yawns.

She shakes her head. "Back in a sec," she says.

I watch her walk a few steps down the bank. When she reaches the water, she hops her way from boulder to boulder. She waves to the kids. Then, before I know it, she's on the rope swing fully dressed, with her miniature admirers cheering as she swings out, farther than any of them, over the river.

She drops feet-first into the water.

Her head breaks the surface a few steps from shore, and she emerges like some sort of water goddess, droplets glistening on her arms, rivulets streaming from her hair, T-shirt suctioned to her body. I don't know how those Renaissance guys painted perfect breasts all the time. They must have had permanent erections.

By the time Sam has picked her way toward me, the

cheers of her groupies are dying down. I wrap her cold body in a bear hug and hope she doesn't notice my Renaissance issues.

"You should jump." She grins. "I dare you."

Lucas laughs, as if she's suggested something impossible.

I think it's the laugh that gets me. And the way Sam raises her eyebrow.

Before I can think too much about it, I stride down the bank toward the rope. With Lucas whooping and Sam cheering, I grab high, run and swing. As I arc over the river, it feels like flying.

Then the water sucks the breath from my lungs and turns my entire body to ice. It's like I'm back in Kootenay Lake learning to swim with Judith, while Dad barks at us about the sturgeons that will eat our toes if we don't kick harder.

My feet touch the rocky bottom and push. With two or three strokes, I'm scraping the shore.

"Crap, that's cold!"

Lucas shakes his head, laughing. "I can't believe you did it, man."

Sam squeezes me, as if she might be able to wring me out.

I'm dripping and possibly hypothermic, but my skin is tingling and, for once, it's not just because Sam is so close.

"I learn new things about you every day, Zac Mawson," she says.

I grin at her.

I've never learned another person before, and no one's learned me. I've never sat on a riverbank and listened to a girl's stories. I've never looked for ways to make her laugh.

As we stretch out on the bank, she tucks her head into my shoulder and closes her eyes. After a while, Lucas begins to snore softly behind us. We're spread out to dry in the sun like a handful of bud.

With my arm around Sam, staring up at the evergreen branches lining the river, I can almost imagine us in the loft of our own cabin with boughs brushing the roof and leaf-mottled sunlight streaming in the windows. We could spend entire days naked, and no one would know. We could climb onto our roof, smoke up and trace patterns in the stars. I could paint her over and over again, the way Alex Colville painted his naked wife standing on her head.

"Can you stand on your head?" I whisper.

"Not right this second," Sam says in a half-asleep voice.

I could hike to my parents' place every couple of days, help out with Walt and with the grow. Judith could stay with us sometimes. Though we'd have to get dressed on those days.

Sam dozes beside me as I build an entire fantasy forest in my head.

•

In the first week of June, it rains as if it will never stop. Dad's in the drying shed weaving twigs into funnel-shaped fish traps. Mom hums to herself while she patches a shirt. Walt has his usual outbursts from the corner. And I sit at the table, papers spread around me, trying to study for my final math exam.

Walt's curses seem strangely appropriate.

$$\log_6(216) + \frac{\log_4(64) - \log_6(6)}{\log_7(49)}$$

"Fucking prick."

Find the value of the constant a for which (e,2) lies on the graph of y=ln(ax).

"Fucking prick."

I'm used to the rhythm of it by the time Walt drifts off in his chair. After a while, Mom's humming stops, too.

It's actually harder to concentrate in silence. I find myself staring at Walt rather than at my notebook, imagining a graph that tracks his years in the woods along one line and his mental decline on another. Those two lines would start in distant corners, then grow slowly closer, and finally cross.

Or I could paint it in a triptych. The first panel would show his glory years, the second would be him and Dad managing on their own, the third could be today, with him slumped in the corner. Though there would be no room in a triptych for the years before he crossed the border, or the stage of his life when he learned to draw.

This is the problem with my paintings, even the ones inside my head. They take off in their own directions. At least graph lines go where I point them.

"Do you think if Walt could go back fifty years, he would choose differently?" I whisper to Mom.

Her eyes jump from her sewing.

"I've never considered it," she says. "It's hard to imagine him anywhere but here."

It's true. His face is darkened and weathered from outdoor work, wrinkled like tree bark. With a few days' growth on his chin, he could be a scraggly evergreen draped in lichen.

"I can't imagine him wearing a suit or working in an office."

"Or working for someone else," Mom says.

Even the idea makes me snort.

Boss: Get those reports done.

Walt: Fucking prick.

But did the woods make him like this, or did he choose the woods because he was pre-made for this life?

I try to imagine the perfect person to run a grow-op. Not worried about authority. Walt meets that requirement, sure. Ready for physical labor. Well, he used to be. Able to spend long hours alone. He certainly doesn't seem to crave company.

Dad's the same way. He's been puttering in the drying shed for hours, with only himself and the bears to talk to, and soon he'll return to the cabin looking calm and happy. He's good with his hands. Tough. The only authority he accepts is God's. He was born for life here.

And then there's me.

"Would you have done things differently?"

The question occurs to me suddenly, and I ask before I can chicken out.

Mom looks surprised. "If I'd chosen differently, I wouldn't have you or Judith," she says.

That's not a real answer.

"If you had the same family, but in town?"

She tilts her chin, looking into the distance. "I grew up differently than your dad," she says finally. "I had school, and friends, and church. A life that was busy, but not always happy. Coming here was a refuge."

"A refuge," I repeat.

"Maybe it's gotten harder in the last few years," she says, glancing at Walt. "But this is still home."

I know she's looking at me now, but I keep my eyes on my notebook. Part of me is praying she'll ask the question and part of me is terrified.

She doesn't ask.

Which doesn't keep it from circling in my head. On the day I graduate, can I climb the trail, throw down my pack, start work and not go back? Could Sam? Could she stand a week of rain, caged by cabin walls? Because if she could, we could manage our own grow, have kids, build our own place. I could paint. Maybe she could teach after-school drama classes in town.

I wouldn't be on my own, using the inside of a shed as a canvas.

Walt mutters in his sleep. Above our heads, the rain rattles against the roof. Outside, a bear huffs.

These would be the sounds of our life. No hallway noise. No phones dinging as Sam's friends texted her their nail-polish disasters.

No applause.

This place is the opposite of a theater stage and trying to picture Sam here, in her leopard-print leggings, seems a little crazy.

But love has conquered hurdles before. My mom is living proof.

10

On Saturday morning, Sam drives to the campground and waits for me at the trailhead. When I see her — which I do well before she spots me — her cut-offs and halter-top seem like a costume. Underneath, she looks like a girl who's scared of bears but trying hard not to show it. She scuffs one running shoe in the dirt.

"Hey."

She jumps.

I don't risk leading her anywhere near the grow. Instead, we take a trail that skirts the side of the mountain past a beaver pond. This is the scene that's going to sell Sam on life in the woods: the perfect stillness of water broken by the ripple of a fish and the dip of a swallow.

"It's gorgeous," Sam breathes. Then she slaps at a mosquito.

She insists on leaving the trail and walking through the reeds until the ground is marshy and sucking at our shoes. Maybe she thinks a beaver will pop its head out of the water. There's no sign of them today, though. Just their lodge across the pond. We're trespassers walking the edges of their property line.

I have a sudden image of a beaver-Walt, aiming a shotgun at us from inside the lodge.

Sam slaps at more mosquitoes.

"Why aren't they eating you?" she asks.

They probably are. "I'm immune."

The image in my head for this morning involved Sam and me lying on a patch of grass, which in my mind was much shorter and softer than these beaver pond reeds. There was a splash of sunlight and a lot of skin.

I reach for her, wrap one hand in her hair and breathe girl-smell.

After a few minutes, she pulls away to scratch her legs again.

"You're not loving this place."

"No, I am! It's beautiful," she says. "I guess I'm just in the mood for people today. How far is your house from here?"

I shrug. "It's a bit of a hike."

"Maybe I could meet your mom," Sam says.

She'd love my mom. She might even like the cabin. But even when she leans against me again and her breasts press against my chest and her breath tickles the skin at my neck, I don't entirely lose my mind. There's no way I can take her to the grow. Am I going to introduce her to Dad and the bears? Tell her to duck if she hears Walt grab his gun?

When I shake my head, she presses her lips together.

"It's just…Mom won't be ready. She'll want to impress you and if she's not expecting us…"

It's lame, and Sam knows it.

"Another day," I promise. "Next time they're in town, we'll get together."

They haven't been to town in ages, but it's not impossible. When we were kids and we would grocery shop with Mom, she would occasionally run into someone she knew from her past. It seemed strange, but it was okay. No one got shot.

Sam turns and heads back toward the campground. I trail after her, not sure whether it's safe to speak.

But then, when we're almost there, she looks back at me. "We should go somewhere fun."

Maybe I'm forgiven.

"I brought sandwiches if you want to have a picnic," I say.

"The mosquitoes are killing me."

"Want to go to the lake?" My entire scene could be relocated to the edge of the sand, with the sound of tiny waves lapping. She could press herself against me on the beach towel. My brain shows a quick series of body positions, all of them good.

"Yes!" Sam says. "But not here. Let's go down to Twin Bays. Everybody will be there."

Which is exactly the reason I'd rather not go. But she's already pushing past the huckleberry bushes, their almost-ripe berries bobbing in her wake.

There's no sign of Amir, though I spot his van as we emerge at the campground. His tree is empty, not even his sleeping bag visible on the platform.

Feeling somehow abandoned, I climb into Sam's car.

"We'll go for another hike soon." Now she's talking to me like I'm a toddler. "The beaver pond was amazing. But doesn't it feel like we should have a little fun now?"

Twin Bays is exactly as fun as I expect.

There's no shade. Sand sticks to the backs of my legs, and jet skis drown out any lapping of waves. Sam is quickly surrounded by squealing friends in bikinis, who are fairly amazing to look at, but also like an alien species. When one of them tries to chat, I get overwhelmed by skin and coconut lotion. I only manage monosyllables.

"Cheer up," Sam says eventually, sitting beside me. She's stripped down to her bathing suit and most of her is temptingly bare.

"Guess what? Tuesday's the last day of school for seniors, right? So Brandon's having a party. A graduation bash."

"Great," I say. I'm watching a game of truth or dare a few steps down the beach. One of the girls is licking Tic Tacs from a guy's belly button.

"So you'll come?" Sam's breast touches my shoulder in a highly distracting way. It takes all my focus to figure out what she's talking about.

"I can't."

I don't want to. I don't want to be stuck in that crowd — the same people who are here on the beach, except pressed together and sweatier. I don't want to celebrate, either.

"Can we blow this place? I want to hang out with you, not with —" I wave one hand at the masses.

"We just got here!"

Her lips curl into a little-girl pout. I can tell she's unhappy with me, but right at this moment, I'm not sure if I care. I've got sweat rolling down my back, sand and a cigarette butt stuck to my elbow.

"I've got to go," I tell her.

"Fine."

She gives me a quick peck, but she doesn't wait for me to leave before joining the truth-or-dare game. As I backtrack across the sand, I can hear her taking over, changing the rules. There's going to be a round entirely of dares, followed by one entirely of truths.

That's one game I'll never be able to play.

When I get to the parking lot, I realize we came in Sam's car. I refuse to turn around and ask for a ride home, though, so I stand on the side of the highway with my thumb out until an extremely large angler picks me up. Then I sit in his Subaru with a tackle box by my feet and a can of worms in my lap.

It's not entirely what I had planned for today.

•

I don't see Sam again until noon on Monday, when she catches up to me on the way to the parking lot and leaps onto my back, wrapping her arms around my neck.

I've been having long imaginary discussions with Sam since Saturday. I call her a social butterfly, and she tells me I'm a hermit. I tell her I want to live in a cabin in the woods, and she laughs as if I'm joking. None of those conversations ever ends well.

But now, when she hops from my back and smiles up at me like the world is perfect, it's tricky to remember why I've been mad.

"Where you going, Zac?"

"I have some paintings stored at my sister's place, and I need to choose a few for Mr. Pires."

"I'll help," she says.

"It'll be boring."

But she insists. When Sam insists on something, with her eyes wide, her mouth in a tiny pout and her fingers half stroking, half prodding my chest, she's impossible to resist.

Soon we pull down the orchard drive, and my sister comes out to meet us.

"I've heard so much about you," Judith gushes, just as Sam says how happy she is to finally meet her. Then Sam squeals over the bus.

"It's so adorable," she says. "And it's on wheels. You could go anywhere!"

Judith grins, but she doesn't exactly look ready for a cross-country adventure. She's puffy-eyed and pale.

"Everything okay?"

She shoos me away with one hand. "No big deal. Can I get you two some lunch?"

When she hears why we've come, she helps me drag my plastic bins from beneath the bus. Soon she and Sam are unrolling one painting after another, as if they're on a private tour of my psyche.

Earlier this year, I created a whole series of imaginary cities. Buildings like mushrooms. Sometimes multi-colored and cubist. Sometimes full of sweeping blue-and-white curves like Mediterranean markets in outer space. The cities are all empty, because I can't imagine what kind of people or creatures might live in buildings that lean and sway like these.

Judith sits beside Sam on the orchard grass. They're both staring at one particular canvas, which isn't even my best. It's the silhouette of a skyline at dusk, sunset glowing pink and purple in the background. Some of the buildings are skyscrapers like the ones you see in photos of New York. But here and there are unusual shapes. Something between a mosque and a giant birdcage with a door swinging open, gilded edges glinting in the last light. Two teardrop-shaped domes connected by an arched walkway.

A tower of egg-shaped shadows balanced on top of one another. Above it all, a single crow.

"Amazing," Sam says softly.

"It's my favorite, too," Judith says. She's only half-looking at the painting, though. My sister keeps darting glances from Sam to me, then grinning behind Sam's back.

"Where do you get your ideas?" Sam asks.

"Obviously not from real life," Judith says. "Do you know this guy has never been more than an hour from here?"

They make matching cartoon faces of astonishment.

"We should go," Sam says immediately, turning to me. "Vancouver road trip!" She practically flings my canvas into the air. I take it from her fingers and reroll it.

"Seriously, Zac. This weekend. I'll tell my dad I'm sleeping over at someone's house. We'll take your truck. If we skip school Friday, we can be in Vancouver that night. Spend Saturday there and head back Sunday."

She makes it sound as if escape is one well-laid plan away.

"Not likely." I turn to Judith. "Can I make grilled cheese for all of us?"

But the girls follow me inside, and Sam won't stop talking. Even as I butter bread and turn on the hot plate, she's babbling about the beach in Vancouver, and collecting shells, and seeing a play at the York. She slides onto the orange bench behind Judith's fold-out table.

"It'll be so much fun."

When I don't respond, she turns to my sister.

"Don't you think he should go? It's criminal to paint like that without seeing a real city."

"I agree. You should go, Isaac," Judith says, putting a bowl of chips on the table and settling herself beside Sam.

I shoot her a glare. She knows I can't skip town for the weekend with Corporal Ko's daughter. What if he came after us? Or what if Dad found out I was in Vancouver? I may as well tell him I was in the third circle of hell for a short vacation.

"Broaden your horizons," Judith says.

I bang a lid onto the pan. It's so convenient that my sister, the one who abandoned her family, now recommends escape as good therapy for everyone. But of course I can't say this in front of Sam.

And what am I doing here anyway, gathering materials for a useless portfolio?

I grit my teeth.

Sam nudges my hip with hers. "Say yes. It'll be amazing."

I take a deep breath. Remove the lid and flip each sandwich, which isn't easy in Judith's small frying pan. I concentrate on squishing them all in.

"We wouldn't even need to pay for a hotel room. Just camp out in the back of the truck. Sleep under the stars…"

I'm pulling dishes from Judith's cupboard when I lose my grip. Literally. One of the plates hits the edge of the counter, and shards fly everywhere. I practically throw the other two onto the table.

I had a picture in my head this past weekend, of Sam falling in love with the forest and deciding to live with me on our own grow. And, okay, I get now that it was a fairy tale. A ridiculous, never-never land option. But she and Judith are rubbing salt on that ripped-up dream with every word they say.

"I can't! I can't go, all right? So get off my case." I can barely see. Red pounds in my head and foams into my line of sight. I crunch across the floor and out of the bus, slamming the door behind me.

I'm between the rows of apple trees before I calm down enough to breathe. I lean on my knees and concentrate.

Inhale, exhale. It takes a lot to rile me, generally. Apparently, it takes a dual attack by Sam and my sister.

Judith once told me that her psychology class had to put their problems into imaginary picture frames, then examine them from a distance. So that's what I do. I settle onto the grass and paint a mental picture of Sam. I imagine her by the creek with our cabin in the background.

But then Hazel pokes her nose into the frame. And next thing you know, my dad shows up in the foreground. *Vancouver? What the hell ya thinkin'?*

My frame has basically splintered by the time I hear the bus door bang. Sam looks around, spots me in the orchard and picks her way through the long grass. She sends clover flowers swaying and bees circling. She could be from a Renoir painting.

"Judith told me about your family," she says, plopping herself on the grass.

I shift my eyes to the bus. What did Judith tell her?

"I didn't know your grandpa was still in such bad shape," Sam says. "You should have said something. I understand if your parents need you around." She tugs on my elbow. "I wouldn't have been so pushy."

I shrug, haul myself up and start back toward the truck. Sam follows, a hand still on my arm.

"I'm trying to apologize," she says.

I stop and turn toward her. "Would you ever live in a cabin in the woods? With an outhouse? And no other people?"

She looks at me as if I've lost my mind.

"Never mind. It's just that..."

"Is that what you're painting next? We could check out some cabins, for inspiration." She says this with a suggestive wiggle of her eyebrows.

Which does make me smile.

None of this is Sam's fault, I remind myself. I'm the one leading a double life.

Sam stands on her tiptoes and plants a kiss on my lips.

"C'mon," she says. "Let's get your paintings."

As we reach the bus door, Judith emerges with a stack of foil-wrapped sandwiches.

"I figured you'd be running out of time," she says.

I take them, along with a collection of forest paintings and three of my skyline canvases. Sam and Judith both insist I take the one with skyscrapers and birdcage buildings. I choose two others — one a market scene with all sorts of strange products and produce for sale, and the other a city along the water, where the buildings above are normal but their reflections are funhouse-warped.

Once Sam and I climb into the truck, Judith wraps her fingers around my window edge and peers at me.

"You going to be okay?"

When I nod, she taps the side of the truck twice, a quick goodbye, and turns back to her bus. No big emotional scene. She gets it, even if she did gang up against me for a while.

"You want to talk about anything?" Sam says, reaching to twine her fingers through the hair at my collar.

Sam, on the other hand, doesn't get it at all.

•

After school on Tuesday, Mr. Pires photographs my paintings one after another, while I have silent convulsions beside him. As soon as he sets up the lights, my brushstrokes begin to look like tsunami-sized mistakes. I see ways my compositions could be improved, if only I could start from scratch. One of my forest scenes makes me think I must have been high on Dad's pot fumes when I painted it.

"I could choose different ones," I say, when Mr. Pires is on his fourth or fifth photo and I can't stand it any longer.

"Hmmm?" he says, still concentrating on his focus.

"I could do different ones. The deadline is gone anyway. I have time." All the time in the world.

He looks up, rubbing his eyes. "These are good, Isaac. Really good. If you'd submitted them six months ago, you'd be holding an acceptance letter right now."

Does art school offer lifetime deferments? I want to throw up.

"I've been hesitant to ask this," Mr. Pires says, leaning over his camera again. "Partly because I don't want to get your hopes up, and partly because of what happened with the magazine — "

"Sorry," I mutter.

"Not your fault," he says easily. "But I have a friend at Emily Carr University. I could send him these. See if there's anything he can do."

I collapse into a desk and put my head in my hands. I don't know why I'm bothering with a portfolio in the first place. But if I'm never going to submit it, why do these photos seem like such a big deal?

"Do they have art classes at the community college here?" I ask through my fingers.

Mr. Pires snorts. "For bored senior citizens, yes."

I dig my fingernails into the skin of my scalp. "Okay."

"Okay what?"

"Okay, send them. Please."

I feel as if one of the tree trunks from my paintings has fallen from the canvas and crushed me. I can't breathe. I can't even begin to process what I've just said.

I stumble out of the building. I don't even remember until I'm driving away that today was the last full day of school. Only exams are left. My days in class are over.

•

I haul a batch of new hoses up the mountain and spend the evening replacing a piece of our watering system, but the job's done long before dark. It's too early to light the lanterns, but the cabin seems dim and the ceiling even lower than usual, like we're living in an underground den.

Grabbing my sketchbook, I take off for the cathedral, Hazel lumbering along behind me. I settle myself on a patch of moss and try to draw the trees, the way the last bits of sunlight slice between them. The way the tips of the branches appear so fragile and so strong at the same time. The way the trunks stretch and split and stretch again.

On paper, they turn into a crumbling civilization, towers toppling against one another and smoke spiraling from the ground.

Nearby, Hazel rips and noses her way into a dead log, her claws shredding the wood and her pink tongue vacuuming insects.

Usually when I draw, my brain drops into a different zone and I think about nothing except pencil and paper.

Time stretches like the evergreens. But now I find myself staring at Hazel, or the leaves, or nothing.

Brandon's party is tonight. Maybe I should have agreed to go with Sam. Half of me hates the idea. The other half of me wants to spend every possible minute with her, making her laugh. Watching the way she scrunches the spikes on her forehead at the same time she scrunches her nose, whenever she's listening hard.

I'm supposed to be enjoying life a little. Maybe I need to take up Buddhist meditation. Live in the present.

Become a druid.

Hazel looks up at the sound of my laugh. I can just imagine what Dad would say if I embraced druidism. Or Buddhism, for that matter.

Mr. Pires said he'd send in my paintings tonight. The files are probably gone by now. I imagine his friend receiving them, maybe posting them somehow to an internal system so admissions committee members (I picture them in black dress shirts and wire-rimmed glasses) can download the files.

And then what? Do they roll their eyes as they flip through? Do they burst out laughing at a turnip-shaped building, and know immediately that I've never actually seen a city?

Or maybe a committee member — one might be enough — stops on a slide to notice the sun glaring from a dome. Maybe she's caught by the way a cat, the sole sign of life, is disappearing down a dark alleyway in the lowest, darkest corner of the piece. She's so intrigued by the painting that she convinces everyone to bend the rules. Such rare talent. I *must* be allowed into the program, she says.

I shake my head and scribble a looping spiral over my disaster sketch. I could go crazy trying to guess people's reactions. Who knows what they're looking for? Maybe they don't like forests and cities. Maybe they're looking for farm life this year. Or even a certain kind of brushstroke.

Maybe it's way, way too late.

When Hazel pads over, I lean against the musky stink of her fur and try to see the world like she does — food and hunger, friend and foe. Then I give up on that, too, and haul myself up and back to the house.

Walt's dozing. Mom's mixing teas. Dad's outside somewhere. I try to read a couple of paragraphs of a book Judith gave me. It's about these guys who saved paintings during World War II, but it's all biography and history and not enough action.

Mom appears behind me, putting a soft hand on my back.

"Why don't you go out for a while?" she suggests. "Go for a drive. Head into town."

"It's too late. I won't get back before dark."

"Could you stay at Judith's?"

"You don't need me?"

"We'll manage." Then she smiles. "I do remember being seventeen."

It's like she's thrown open my cage door. I didn't even know that this was what I wanted, but I feel a million times lighter. I give Mom a quick kiss on the cheek and toss a change of clothes into my pack.

Then I'm out the door before she changes her mind. Or before Walt wakes up or Dad arrives to change her mind for her.

11

Once I find a place to park along the gravel shoulder, I cut the engine. Immediately, the sounds of the party pour in. There's music blaring and guys shouting, with an extra-loud laugh erupting every once in a while, or a sudden whoop.

I resist the urge to drive away again. Instead, I get out of my truck. I take a deep breath and climb the steps to the porch, where I shoulder my way between groups of drunk people.

"Isaac!" Lucas's voice reaches out like a big hand. He's sprawled on the couch in the living room, looking, as usual, slightly too cool for the place. Soon I have a beer in my hand to take the edge off my sweaty claustrophobia.

"Happy to see you here, bud. This isn't your usual scene." He's buzzed his hair short, maybe to match his black T-shirt with the sleeves cut off.

"Heard it was the party of the year."

He laughs. "They say that about every party. And if you miss one, they make it sound like you were left out of the greatest night ever. But they're all the same, really."

He has to shout to be heard over the music. As I scan the crush of bodies, I try to imagine hanging out at these places all the time. There's a very drunk girl dancing on the dining-room table. Another girl is pushing her way from the room, mascara running down her cheeks. There's a skinny dude swaying in one corner, looking as if he's about to hurl.

Watching this every week sounds like torture.

I'm shoved aside by a massive guy in a muscle shirt. "Lucas! My car's crapped out, man, and I gotta pick someone up. Can you take a look?"

"No problem." Lucas extracts himself from the couch cushions.

I resist the urge to throw myself at his ankles as he leaves. Maybe he notices.

"Back in a flash," he says.

As soon as he's gone, the music seems louder and the beer fumes thicker. I climb onto the back of the couch and scan the crowd for Sam. There's no sign of her, so I head for the patio.

Halfway there, I'm almost bowled over by two drunk guys grappling. A lamp crashes to the floor. I manage to get past, but it feels like squeezing myself into a solid wall of people, everyone shouting now.

"Look out!" someone yells. A dining-room chair tips over.

I try to step forward and get an elbow in my ribs. I'm not even sure I'm still heading in the direction of the patio doors.

But it doesn't matter. Because at that moment, Sam finds me.

"Zac! You came!"

As she throws herself toward me, I get a whiff of wine and cinnamon gum.

"You okay?" she shouts in my ear.

"I need space!"

The chaos fades as soon as we get outside. Sam leads me around the corner of the house and we sit against the siding. Just enough light reaches us to make the edges of her skin glow.

"Whew," I say. "Getting out wasn't easy."

"Try getting out of *my* house," she says. "My dad threw a fit. House parties apparently don't fit with his vision for my future."

"And what's his vision?"

"RCMP officer, like him," she says, as if this should be obvious.

"Seriously?"

"He seems to think it's hereditary," she says. "Programmed into my DNA."

She curls against me and lets her head rest on my chest. I wrap my arms around her, wanting to pull her impossibly close.

"I don't see it." This may be my own genetic code talking, because my gut cramps up whenever Sam mentions the RCMP. I try to think objectively, but I still can't imagine her as a cop. Police officers are supposed to be cool and collected at all times. Sam is more an explosion of random energy.

"He alternates between ignoring me and suffocating me," she's saying now. "No wonder my mom left."

I listen while she tells me about their argument. It was probably no different than a million other arguments between dads and their daughters. But in Sam's mind, it's like a stone stacked on other stones and the whole wall seems about to cave in on her.

Maybe we're all trying to avoid our own cave-ins. Maybe at these parties, the gates in the walls lift for a couple of hours. Maybe everyone's looking for a temporary emotional leave of absence just like me.

"I've never been so happy to see him leave for a night shift," Sam says. Then she tugs down the neckline of my shirt and kisses the skin beneath. "I'm sorry I pressured you to come tonight. I know it's not your scene."

As if on cue, a beer bottle flies from the deck and shatters against the back fence.

Sam raises her head and I raise my eyebrows.

She laughs. "Want to get out of here?"

"Where to?"

"Dad's on night shift, remember?"

We get to her house in record time. And once inside, we don't even make it to the bedroom. She strips off my shirt in the entranceway and steps out of her jeans on the living-room carpet.

My skin feels as if there's an electric current running through it. Sam grins at me as if she knows things I don't. Which is true.

Suddenly, I'm nervous. I'm worried about what I smell like or taste like or look like. When I produce the condom (stolen weeks ago from Judith's drawer), the crinkling of the package seems amplified in the semi-dark. But then Sam's kissing me again and I forget to worry. Her lips slide to my neck. I press hard against her. My breath seems loud in my ears and hers is just as loud against my skin.

The garage door is exponentially louder.

Sam swears as she rolls off me.

I'm frozen in the dark. My lungs refuse to operate.

"I think you might want your clothes," Sam whispers. She sounds almost as if she's laughing, but maybe my ears are frozen, too.

"Go," she says.

I scramble for my pants. My belt is undone but I leave it that way. On the other side of the house, a door squeaks. I snatch my shirt from the entranceway, fling open the front door and dive outside. I practically hurl myself off the entrance stoop and into the shadow of the house.

My truck is here. Of course Corporal Ko has seen my truck.

But who cares? Because my shirt is on now, and thank God my keys are in the pocket of my jeans. I can turn the ignition and escape.

I've been driving for ten minutes before I realize I'm heading in exactly the wrong direction.

How do these things happen to me?

My face burns every time I replay my escape. I just want to get home.

I round the final curve, but as I'm about to pull off the highway, I spot a car in front of the logging-road gate.

Someone's parked there.

I don't stop to see whether it's a broken-down car or a traveler taking a late-night nap. Instead I drive ahead, pull a U-turn and double back to the campground. I cut the engine and wrap myself in an old blanket from behind my seat.

I spend the night in a half-doze, not sure if I'm awake or dreaming. And when I finally pry my eyes open at dawn and take stock of my numb toes and frozen nose, I know one thing.

I don't like running and hiding.

•

The strange car is gone by the time I drive back to our logging road, so I make it up the mountain for breakfast and a shower. But then I head back into town. Dad needs me to meet with a contact. Plus I made the mistake of mentioning that Judith looked tired, and now Mom wants to send her wild ginger. Enough to feed a small village for a year.

As I reach cell reception, my phone buzzes and buzzes with texts from Sam. But I don't answer. I haven't figured out whether I'm embarrassed or mad. Or if I'm overreacting and the entire situation should be funny. Maybe this is another version of the lipsticked locker?

But no, I think I'm angry. She said her dad was working night shift.

Every time I remember the sound of the garage door, my insides shrivel.

When the phone buzzes again, I turn it off and shove it into my pocket.

It's early afternoon by the time I pull into the bar parking lot. I find Judith inside dusting window ledges, though the place seems to suit a thin layer of dust. The carpet is an orange and brown pattern, the tables are wood laminate, and the walls are hung with wagon wheels and beer signs. Even the few guys slouched at the tables look past-due.

My sister's the only clean thing in this place.

"What are you doing here?" she says. "Other than breaking liquor laws and trying to get me fired?"

I drop the wild ginger on the counter. "Came to say hello. Make sure you're okay."

"Of course I'm okay," she says.

She's gone back to her dusting, so she says this to the window ledge more than to me.

"You didn't look okay last week."

Between Sam choosing canvases and my mini-meltdown, I never did find out what was bothering my sister.

"Did you and Garrett break up?" I ask, trying not to sound too hopeful.

"He wants me to move in with him," she says.

I groan.

Judith narrows her eyes and turns away to shuttle a new pint to a guy in the corner.

I climb on a bar stool and wait, trying to rephrase my groan more diplomatically.

"You just got your own place," I say when she gets back. "You can't give that up already."

"That bus is like an oven in this heat."

I bite my tongue. Hard.

"He doesn't want me working here anymore. Says there's too many hands and too many eyes."

"What do you think?"

She shrugs. "It's not exactly five-star, is it?"

"You could get another job, easy. One of the restaurants, maybe." Thus I prove it's technically possible for me to be tactful.

"Maybe I wouldn't have to. Garrett has a nice place. Really nice."

She's going to stay in his house and do his laundry? Seriously?

"Garrett's an ass." Diplomacy over.

Judith folds her arms across her chest. "You don't even know him."

"Am I wrong?"

"Did you need something, or did you just come to irritate me?"

"You can't move in with that guy. You may as well move back in with Walt. What the hell, Judith?"

She says nothing. Her jaw is clenched and she's blinking fast. After a minute, she points toward the door.

I slide off the stool.

"I think you should be careful," I say, turning to her one more time.

"Do you have any idea how hard this is? I'm all by myself here. And Garrett may have his faults, but he can be really sweet."

"Yeah. Sweet like Big Bugger. Or Dusky."

She shoves me the rest of the way out the door and slams it closed. For a few minutes I stand on the stoop and contemplate going back in. I come up with multiple ways to say "he's an ass" using different words.

This is unlikely to help.

Eventually I stomp back to the truck and pull out of the parking lot, headed for the viewpoint where my meeting's supposed to take place.

The whole way there, I stew. I don't even know whether to blame Judith and her asshole boyfriend, or Dad and his bears for getting us into this situation. For driving Judith out.

I'm angry at Judith for not sticking up for herself and making her own choices...but who am I to be angry about something like that?

•

Two years ago, Judith was cleaning fish at the edge of the creek when one of the bears — an eccentric old guy named

Dusky — decided the fish should be his. He swiped her long and deep across the back.

The image of Judith staggering into the cabin, shirt and skin in red ribbons, is burned into my eyelids. She wasn't even crying. She was defiant, as if the thing she'd always expected had finally happened.

"What did you do?" That's what Dad yelled.

I think he felt bad about it, after. He tiptoed around the house while Judith lay on her stomach, skin stitched together by Mom and slathered with salve. After a couple days, when she could get up again, Dad was the one who dragged the wicker chair inside and padded it with pillows.

I remember that. Him arranging the pillows. I'm not sure Judith does, though.

I also remember the sound of the shot when he killed the bear. And I remember the size of the hole we had to dig to fit that carcass. None of us could face the thought of eating the meat. Dad had known Dusky a long time.

•

I wheel into the viewpoint along the highway just west of town. Once I've scanned the place to make sure I'm the only one here, I cut the engine. I find a perch in the covered picnic area overlooking the patchwork of farm fields below. There's an interpretive plaque here explaining how the river was diked to allow this "fertile expanse of corn and canola."

I hear the motorcycle long before I see it.

The plaque doesn't say anything about illegal grows or motorcycle gangs.

When he pulls off his helmet, the guy reveals collar-length curly blond hair and cheeks pocked with acne. He's younger than I expected. Younger and cockier.

"You the Mawson kid?" he asks.

I remind myself that we need this guy for the year's profits.

"Isaac," I say, reaching to shake his hand.

He has a firm grip at least. And he gets right to business. "When will you be harvesting?"

"Early if the weather stays like this. Mid-August, maybe."

"I'll give you the number to call when you're ready," he says. I pass him my phone, and he punches in the number for his burner. He shoots me a few more questions about quantity and quality, which I answer automatically.

"What?" he asks then, eyebrows raised.

I realize I'm smirking at him.

I flush, but I tell him the truth. "Just thinking about what we'd be if we were born in a different place, that's all. Maybe you'd be giving me stock tips."

He cracks a smile for the first time. One of his teeth is half-black, rot growing from the root. "Not likely."

He's already climbing back on his bike. I hold up my phone. "I'll call next month and check in."

Our business meeting's over. I wait awhile until the rumble of his Harley fades. Then I climb back into the truck and sit staring over the fields. I'm still thinking about what we'd all be if we were born somewhere different. Somewhere without bears and without weed.

•

When I finally answer one of Sam's texts, she calls me from Burger Barn. She and Lucas are having dinner. So instead of talking about what happened, I slide in beside my girlfriend, who suddenly feels like a stranger, and I act as if everything's perfect.

Sam seems to think that all is forgotten.

"Zac, are you ever going to ask me to grad?" she asks, poking the back of my hand with one of her Burger Barn fries. Across from me, Lucas chuckles.

I feel like a squirrel that's wandered to the edge of our clearing and frozen, knowing it's in dangerous territory.

"You get four tickets," she says. "I could sit with your sister."

"I'm not going," I say.

"What?" She pulls herself upright so she can give me the full benefit of her appalled look.

"Way to crush the establishment, man," Lucas says. He's on his second milkshake. It's quite possible he's stoned again.

"You're going, aren't you?" Sam asks Lucas.

He nods. "The establishment loves me."

"It's a march around the gym in a robe," I protest.

"It's a celebration, Zac," Sam says. "You watch the doors to the world getting thrown open and have a moment of joy." This comes with expansive hand motions.

I move our shakes out of her reach. "I'll have my own moment."

"What about your parents?"

"They don't like to come to town."

"Not even for grad?"

I shrug. "I don't think it's occurred to them."

"What about Judith?" Her questions come like bullets now.

"Judith doesn't care."

"What about the dance after?"

Maybe this is the real problem. "You want to go to the dance?"

"Only with a guy who cares enough to ask me."

Lucas has stayed silent throughout this exchange. When I turn to him for help, he shrugs.

I want to make Sam happy, obviously. So if she wants to go to the dance, I'll take her to the dance. "If you want to go, we'll go."

"I want *you* to want to go," she says.

This entire conversation makes *me* want to poke my eye out with my milkshake straw, but I settle for squishing the innards from a French fry.

"I want to go, with you," I say firmly.

Now that's apparently not good enough.

"Do you even care about the future?" she asks. "I spend half my life dreaming about university and getting out of this place, and you didn't even submit your portfolio on time. You're not going to grad, you have no plans for next year…. It's like you're never going to leave this place."

I feel like that stupid squirrel after Big Bugger caught sight of it.

"My family still needs me around," I say. "Walt's sick. My dad's got a lot of work. Mom can't juggle everything on her own."

Sam stares at me. "You're not freaking Cinderella," she says. "You know there's home care, right? I bet the government even pays for some of it."

"Your dad can hire someone to help out," Lucas offers.

Wanted: employee to live in isolated forest region, guarding agricultural plot. Must be familiar with bears and helicopters.

Experience with mental-health issues an asset. Must have flexible availability. Wages and benefits to be paid in illegal substances.

He should post that in the community newspaper.

Sam's still staring at me. "So that's it. You'll spend forever in the woods."

As if the idea doesn't skewer me every time I think about it.

"Not forever. But I have things to take care of."

She gives a frustrated huff — the type I hear from Hazel when I refuse to share my dinner.

"Excuse me," she says. Then she slides out of the booth and stomps toward the door. She's in combat boots today, which makes the stomping doubly effective.

"Sam!" I call. When she doesn't stop, I run after her. "What am I supposed to do? Make up some plans that will satisfy you? I have issues at home. I'm working on them."

"Sure," she says, throwing her arms in the air, not looking at me.

"Don't you think we have other things to talk about?" I fire back. "You have some issues at your house, too, as I remember."

The glass Burger Barn door swings closed in my face.

"You two had sex, didn't you?" Lucas says when I drop back into the booth.

"What?"

"The tension in here is a serious buzzkill. I guess it didn't go well?"

My mouth opens and closes, but nothing comes out. For the moment, I've turned into Walt.

"We didn't have sex!" It comes out much louder than it should, and several heads turn toward us. My insides twist tighter.

"We *almost* had sex," I whisper.

"None of my business, man," Lucas says. "I just worry you're both going to get hurt. You two are kind of... different."

Then he leaves, too. And I'm stuck in Burger Barn alone, with three half-finished milkshakes, thinking that there may be a few issues with my temporary emotional leave of absence this spring. Girlfriends and the idea of "temporary" aren't as compatible as I once thought.

Did Lucas mean that Sam and I are two different types of people, or did he mean that we're both weird, and we might be compatible because of it?

I finish all three milkshakes before I leave.

The idea of heading up the mountain forever, leaving Sam and Lucas and my rolled-up canvases behind...it doesn't feel right anymore. But the idea of letting Dad harvest by himself and leaving Mom to deal with Walt's moods while chopper blades thwack in the distance...that doesn't seem possible, either.

Maybe I haven't considered grad because grad means decision-making. Maybe Sam's right, and I haven't thought seriously enough about the future.

I remember my resolution of this morning when I woke up in the campground.

No more hiding.

12

I write my math and English finals on Friday. On my way home, I pull into the campground and circle past an RV and a few kids with bikes until I reach the road near the treehouse.

Amir's tarp is in the tree, but there's still no sleeping bag dangling from the edge of the platform. His bucket's gone.

I head for the campsite where Sam and Lucas and I sat with him, smoking up and discussing his place in the universe. When I spot the VW van parked in its same spot, I feel a strange sort of relief.

Maybe as long as Amir's still around, I don't hold the title for most confused.

Then a woman pops up from one of the lawn chairs. She's a bit chubby with blonde hair back-combed above bright blue eyes.

"Sorry," I stammer. I've walked right into her campsite. "I was looking for Amir."

She turns toward the van. "Sweetcheeks? Someone here to see you."

Sweetcheeks?

The side door of the van rolls open and Amir steps out. He wears a giant grin.

"Isaac! A pleasure. I see you've met the love of my life." He stops to give the blonde a squeeze and a long, noisy kiss.

"Just came by to see how you were doing," I say.

He strides over and claps both hands on my shoulders. For a moment I'm worried he's going to hug me. But he simply stares at me, beaming.

"I am about to embark on the next stage of my journey, friend," he says. "Destiny and I, we are going west. We are going to drive until we meet the ocean and we cannot drive any longer."

"Big changes." Could Destiny possibly be her real name?

"One cannot meet the universe in baby steps, friend."

"I guess not." I have to get out of here.

Destiny comes over and wraps her arm around Amir's waist.

"You should tell him how we met, sweetcheeks," she says. "In town that day? It was like fate. For sure."

"Tea?" Amir offers. "Before we talk, yes?"

No. Because I have to go. I have to go before it fully sinks in that even the druid has plans. The druid's getting out of here, on a date with Destiny.

"I just realized...I'm late." Late for my date with the void.

Amir continues to beam.

"Another time," he says. "But don't wait too long. We have a small problem with the van, but as soon as we fix it, Destiny and I are eager to meet our future."

Destiny, Destiny, Destiny.

She has a giggle like a chipmunk's chattering. I can't imagine worse torture than being locked in a VW van with these two, all the way to the coast.

Except maybe having nowhere to go at all.

•

Just as I get home, a chopper sweeps overhead toward the lake.

We've always been aware of the air.

When Judith and I were kids, we used to build elaborate forts in the woods. After combing the forest for a spot where four trees made a rough square, we'd spend all day, or many days, hauling deadwood and downed branches to weave our walls. Then we'd make an evergreen bough roof.

One summer, thanks to two perfectly positioned branches, we even had a loft.

That particular fort was the one to beat all forts. We'd "borrowed" some plastic piping from Dad and rigged running water from the creek to create a kitchen. We'd built an evergreen couch. And after raiding an old hunting camp we'd found on one of our more distant rambles, we even had a second-story roof over the loft — an orange tarp stretched between the tree trunks.

It was a palace.

It was such a good fort that when it was finished, we dragged Mom and Dad through the trees to see it.

"Look at the loft!"

"Running water!"

"Roof!"

But the minute Dad moved, we fell silent. He was like a giant towering over us. He grabbed the tarp and yanked it down so hard that branches snapped and our loft tumbled. We scrambled out of the way.

"What do you think you're doing?" His voice, that quiet, was even worse than yelling. "You put up a bright orange flag in the forest, like a signal for anyone passing overhead to see?"

We stayed silent.

"Are you a couple of idiots? Can you not think?"

Dad stood there while Judith and I took apart every branch of that fort, spreading the pieces through the trees, tears and snot dripping onto the leaves.

I think that's the first time I knew our family was different. That we had secrets. That we weren't like the families in town, or the ones in books. For some reason, we were hiding. We couldn't play fort because we were already involved in some real-life game of hide-and-seek.

•

There's another chopper after church on Sunday. It doesn't travel the same course as the first. It's not big enough to be a logging bird and it's strange to see a helicopter on a Sunday.

Dad figures there's trouble coming.

"We're going to scatter the plants," he announces after lunch. "You and me, Isaac. We'll have to poke around a bit, find the sunniest spots. Put them here and there."

"What about water?"

"We'll have to haul it."

"Fucking prick," Walt says.

For once I agree with Walt. Hauling buckets of water might work for ten plants, but we've got a few hundred. And I'm the one who'll be doing the hauling.

Dad slaps a hand on my shoulder as he makes for the door.

"Little hard work never hurt no one," he says.

Which is not precisely true. Dad's got a messed-up back and Walt's altogether broken.

"Prick," Walt says.

"Indeed."

Mom shoots me a glance, but I ignore her.

Walt leans in suddenly, eyes locked on mine. His mouth opens, closes, his tongue circling his lips the way it does when he's striving for real words.

"Been here…too long," he manages.

"You think?" I don't expect him to answer. We have these pseudo-conversations sometimes, Walt and I, when he manages words. He says something, I reply, and he says something entirely unrelated. It might look like an exchange from a distance, but it's not.

"Gotta go. Move on…to the other slice. No. No. No. Slice." His mouth contorts. "Place," he spits finally.

"Let's not get ahead of ourselves," Mom says. She pours Walt a cup of tea and sits down beside him.

"Signs," Walt says.

I look back and forth between him and Mom. What is he talking about?

His mouth moves frantically again. "Signs don't go away just…because you keep your eyes closed."

It's not exactly the words that make me pause. It's the way he says them. He looks directly at Mom, then at me.

I don't remember when I last heard a sentence this clear from Walt.

He leans in, forearms on the table and one gnarled finger pointing at me. "How long we been here?"

"Ten years, at least." I look at Mom for confirmation, and she nods. Before that we had a squat on some other land a couple hours to the north.

"Grandpa had his eye on this property for years, even when your grandma was still alive," Mom tells me.

"Know other ones," Walt says. "We gotta switch."

That's when Dad swings the door open, banging his boots on the stoop.

"You comin'?" he says.

Walt hauls himself half out of his chair. This time he points his finger at Dad.

"Gotta move." He's almost shouting.

"Nobody's moving." Dad doesn't seem surprised. They must have had this conversation before. "How d'ya think you're getting off this property?" Dad says. "It's a long ways east."

Walt collapses into the chair.

"Fucking prick," he says. But not too loudly. More like he's saying it to himself than to Dad.

I pull on my boots and get ready to haul some plants.

"Does he really have other property?" I ask Dad, once we're away from the walls. "Does he own it, or just know about it?"

Dad grunts. "Never been there."

Communication skills run in our genes, obviously.

The plants are big enough that it's not easy hauling them up and through the trees. Branches reach for me like live things and I'm soon covered in dirt and bits of fern and leaf. Dad is hauling as many as he can, but he'll pay for it tomorrow. I try to outpace him, and I leave him the sunny spots closest to the clearing while I search for those farther away.

Eventually we take a water break, both of us panting. Dad has sword fern in his hair. He looks half-sasquatch.

"You ever think about retiring?" I ask as he lowers himself to the ground beside me. He moves like an old man.

"Retire from what?" he says.

I wave my hand at the clearing.

"You must have some money put away. Do you need to keep doing this?"

Dad looks as if this has never occurred to him.

"We got people waiting for our crop," he says.

"I didn't mean right this minute," I said. "But you could take a break. Have a look at Walt's other property, maybe. Give your back a rest."

Dad takes a long swig of water, wipes his mouth on his sleeve, and then stares at the half-emptied clearing.

"You planning on going somewhere?" he asks.

For a long time, I stare straight ahead, too. It would be so easy to end this conversation right here and pretend it never happened.

"Art school," I manage finally. It comes out sounding like a question.

Slowly, Dad turns his head toward me. He looks as if I may be an imposter. Or an alien.

"What the hell are you going to do with art school?"

And I have no idea what to say, because I've never once thought beyond the part where I go away.

"Dumb idea, I guess," I mumble.

"Damn right," Dad says.

I get up pretty quickly after that, and go back to the plants. Dad sits in the dirt and watches me haul the first one into the trees. When I return to collect another, he's disappeared.

There's a dull, steady pain beneath my ribs.

•

A bell should sound as I set down my pen down after Monday's history exam. That's the last one. I go straight from the gym to the office, where I cough up the money for two tickets to the graduation dance. It feels like buying tickets to my own waterboarding, but whatever.

"Don't run away too quick," the secretary says as she hands me the tickets. "Mr. Pires wants to see you."

I deliver the dance tickets to Sam and leave her squealing happily, our Burger Barn argument forgotten. Then I head for the art room.

As soon as Mr. Pires looks up at me, I know. I almost turn and walk straight back out of the room.

"I heard from my contact at Emily Carr," he says, handing me a copy of an email.

...potential...unique point of view...unfortunately...waitlists...bureaucracy...following year.

I shove the paper into my back pocket.

"It was a long shot." Maybe my voice is a little flat, but I hold it together.

"I don't want this to discourage you," Mr. Pires said. "There are other great programs out there, and there's always next year."

"Sure."

I'm one of those massive granite boulders that hulks among the trees, left over from a previous ice age. I'm stone.

And I want out of the art room so badly I could single-handedly shift tectonic plates.

"Thanks for trying. I've got to go. I'm supposed to meet someone — "

"Come by anytime," Mr. Pires calls after me. "We'll figure out a plan."

But I'm already gone.

Walking through the halls, I can feel my edges crumbling. Chunks are falling from me. I focus on getting to the foyer, getting to Sam and getting out of here. We'll climb into my truck and we'll park beside the lake somewhere and I'll stare at the waves until my chest stops feeling like it's going to implode and —

"Zac! Are you ready?"

She's standing with a group of her friends. They wave at me like a team of synchronized swimmers.

"I told them we're going up the lake and now everyone wants to come. It's a party." She smiles, as if this is a good thing.

The chasm widens beneath my rib cage.

"I'll drive up with you, then catch a ride back to town with the girls," she says.

I'm silent all the way to the truck, but she doesn't seem to notice. It's only once we're pulling onto Canyon Street and she's finished waving through the rear window at her carful of followers that she puts a hand on my shoulder.

"You okay?"

I don't want to talk about it now. Not with the girls behind us honking at each red light, their car practically bouncing with their energy.

I shore up whatever edges I have left. "Fine. Just tired."

"I know," Sam says. "I had the most exhausting day, too."

I don't hear the rest of her story. I nod when she pauses, and that seems to be enough.

As soon as we arrive at the lake, she breaks out a water

bottle full of mixed booze, stolen from her dad's supplies. She passes it around.

"He doesn't notice when you do this?" one of the girls asks. "My dad marks the level on his bottles."

Sam rolls her eyes.

When the bottle passes my way, I take a swig. It tastes like lava, but it helps a little. Then I sit on the beach and watch the girls swim, wishing I had Sam to myself.

I think back to the morning I met her in the auditorium, after she lipsticked my locker. She had a spotlight personality, she said then.

At the time, I didn't recognize the implications.

13

The junior band squeaks and honks its way through a series of ceremonial marches.

Judith insisted I attend tonight. There would be only one high-school graduation in my entire life, she said. If I didn't go, I might regret it for decades. After all the work I'd put in, I deserved a moment of celebration.

So here I am.

Apparently there's been an epic graduation scene on some TV show this week. Around me, everyone's whispering about it. I grin as if I love the show, too, but I have no idea what they're talking about. It's a relief when our line inches forward.

I spot Sam in the audience. Judith has to work, which is ridiculous after all the effort she put into getting me here. Still, I shuffle after Lucas, trying not to swish my robe too much. Then I march across the stage.

It doesn't feel like Judith said it would. When the principal puts the diploma in my hand, it's the same as when Mr. Pires handed me the art school email.

I join the line of students on the benches at the other

side of the stage. When Lucas gets there, he's blinking fast. Maybe it felt like it was supposed to, for him.

After the ceremony, his dad, tall and thin in a stylish black suit, shakes his hand.

"It's a start, I'll say that," he says.

I want to punch him.

Lucas's mom looks like a plump chocolate-chip cookie in her shiny polka-dotted dress. She wraps her arms around him.

"You did it," she says.

Lucas smiles — the broadest, most sincere smile I've ever seen. I think of Sam's description of the prison doors swinging open, and I can imagine Lucas diving for those doors.

Then, suddenly, my dad's shaking my hand, too.

"What the..."

And Mom's wrapping her arms around me, squeezing tight.

"What are you doing here?"

In her cotton Sunday dress, she looks hopelessly old-fashioned. Dad wears dress pants and a buttoned shirt I've never seen before.

"Judith arranged it." Mom sniffs. Even Dad looks a little bleary-eyed. And before I know it, I'm all watery, too.

And confused.

"Where's Walt?"

"Judith's staying with him for the evening."

That's what almost tips me over the edge. I have to turn away, squeeze my eyes shut and take a deep breath before I regain control.

Lucas's dad turns toward us and congratulates me. There are introductions. Lucas's parents shake the hands of mine, and our moms somehow discover, in their first three sentences, that they both love to garden. They exchange tips on a parasitic fly.

I've stepped into a parallel universe.

Lucas's family has dinner reservations. As they leave, I stare at my parents, wondering what I'm supposed to do with them.

"We have Judith's car and she left us dinner at her place," Mom says.

I don't know what I'll do first when I see my sister. Kiss her, or kill her.

No wonder she said I had to be here. She'd already planned the whole thing.

"I believe she's arranged for your friend Sam to join us."

I may kill her.

But Mom looks so happy. She's glowing. Even Dad is puffed up like a partridge.

"Did you get a haircut?" I ask incredulously.

He grunts, while steering Mom out of the gym.

As soon as we push open the door of Judith's bus, a waft of lasagna greets us. There's a small foil pan in the toaster oven, with a loaf of bread and a huge bowl of salad on the counter beside it. She's draped the table in a white cloth and folded origami napkins atop four white plates. A bottle of red wine serves as the centerpiece.

When Sam arrives and Dad opens the door for her, his brows shoot up. But she's fairly conservatively dressed, for Sam. She's wearing a strapless green-and-white checked dress with a thin green streak in her hair to match.

She introduces herself and shakes their hands. She compliments Mom's necklace.

For a brief moment, I think everything's going to be okay.

Then, as soon as Dad finishes grace and we fill our plates, she starts talking about my art.

"He does the most amazing paintings I've ever seen."

"He's been drawing since he could hold a pencil," Mom says. "When he was a toddler, his granddad taught him how to draw people, and he was off. He skipped right over the stick-figure stage."

I have no memory of this, obviously, and I find it difficult to imagine Walt teaching a toddler to draw. Besides, I'd rather not talk about art at the moment. Or ever.

Dad scoops another serving of salad and we both bend our heads over our plates.

"Speaking of paintings," Sam says, as if we were all doing so. "I made you a present."

She pops up, reaches into her bag and pulls out a wrapped rectangle.

I open it reluctantly. It could be a picture of the two of us. Or something else that will prove embarrassing to open in front of my parents.

But it's not.

It's a small hardcover book. The front is a glossy reproduction of one of my forest paintings. Inside, page after page is filled with my work.

It looks real. It looks like an art book you might find in a store.

I turn it over in my hands. "How did you do this?"

"I begged Mr. Pires to give me the files," she says. "I practically had to sign in blood to convince him I would use them for this and only this. I ordered it online."

There's a photo of me on the back flap, one that Sam snapped on her phone at the viewpoint.

"Thank you," I manage. "This is the nicest thing…"

"I knew you'd love it!" she squeals. "And I wanted to make sure my gift was the best."

Which is entirely, undeniably Sam. But at this moment, I can only grin at her.

Mom reaches for the book and slowly turns the pages.

"They're wonderful," she says after a few minutes. "When did you paint all of these?"

"You haven't seen them?" Sam says incredulously.

Mom passes the book to Dad. When he doesn't take it, she sets it on the tablecloth near his arm.

Sam turns to me. "You have to show them the city paintings, Zac. I didn't put those ones in the book. Are they still in the storage space?"

"I don't know if this is — "

"They're brilliant," Sam tells my parents. "All these creepy buildings. You've got to see them."

"Another time," Dad says.

Sam falls silent.

"More bread, anyone?" Mom asks.

When no one answers, the silence feels stretched and sticky, like paint left too long on a palette. I get up from the table and start the dishes. As I wash, I try not to listen too closely to Sam talking about drama, and her theater school plans, and — God help us all — her father's job.

It's Dad's fault. He asks.

"He's a watch commander at the detachment," she says easily. "It's a lot of shift work."

"Does he. . . ." Dad has to stop to clear his throat. "Does he enjoy the work?"

I've stopped washing. I stand with a sudsy plate in my hand, watching the table from the corner of my eye.

"I guess so," Sam says.

"Well, that was delicious," Mom says. "I wonder if Judith's left dessert in the fridge."

But Dad stands. "Think I've had enough for one night." He gives me a long, searching look as if I might be someone he doesn't know.

Then the door swings firmly closed behind him.

Sam, wide-eyed, looks from me to Mom and back again.

"I suppose it's time," Mom says. She gives me a kiss on the cheek.

"Wonderful to meet you," she tells Sam.

Then she's gone, too. I can feel Sam's eyes on me, and I'm as twisted up as a wrung-out dishcloth.

"Wow," she says.

I stack the plates carefully in the drying rack.

"He's not exactly a barrel of laughs, is he?"

There's almost a repeat of the grilled cheese incident. A plate almost hits the floor. I'm so wound up that I'm not even sure who to be angry with. But the book saves me. Because when I turn to look at Sam, I spot the book on the tablecloth and I see the time she took to make this day special.

"Forget them," I tell her, forcing my lungs to expand and my fists to unclench. "Let's go to this dance of yours."

She smiles.

When she goes into the bathroom to freshen up, I twist the cap from Judith's unopened bottle of wine and take a giant swig.

Sam emerges with cherry red on her lips and glitter in her hair. "Ready?"

"We'd better walk. I'm taking this for the road," I say, my hand around the neck of the bottle.

"Perfect." Sam laughs.

Which for some reason makes me want to cry. But I squeeze my eyes tight one more time, take another swallow and pull her out the door. Because according to my sister, there's only one graduation night in my whole life. And I may as well get it over with.

•

We wade into a sea of guys in suits and girls wearing shiny dresses. I ditched the empty wine bottle along the way, so now we drink the chemical-scented mix that Sam smuggled into the gym in her hairspray bottle. We dance (or Sam dances while I attempt to sway in some sort of acceptable rhythm). When we escape outside for air, we find Lucas sitting on the gravel staring at the stars.

"Lost your date?" I ask him. He's supposed to be here with one of Sam's friends.

"I...uh...hit a raccoon on the way here, and she's not speaking to me."

It seems as good a time as any to break out the bud. After all, this is my once-only graduation. Isn't that what everyone's been telling me?

I pull a joint from the breath mint case in the inside pocket of my suit jacket and, after a quick glance to either side, I light up, suck deeply and pass it along.

"It's better than that crap you smoked with the druid," I tell Sam.

Draft Dodger Dark is like a slow expansion of reality. And this is the very best of last year's crop.

Soon all three of us are lying on our backs, staring into the sky.

"Speaking of the druid," Lucas says, ten minutes after I actually mentioned him. "I fixed Amir's van."

"How did that happen?"

"I saw him driving through town with this girl, but his van was squealing like a dying animal."

"And you fixed it? Nice work," Sam says.

"Fan belt."

"I saw him a couple days ago. He's leaving soon," I muse.

"Gone," Lucas says. "He's skipped town with Destiny."

Which makes all three of us crack up, until at last Sam pulls herself together with a long breath, tilts her head to the sky and says, "I had no idea there were so many stars in the universe."

I could float into those stars and drift there forever. Sam's fingers rest lightly on the back of my hand. I can feel Lucas on my other side. I wish I had a cell number for the druid. I could tell him I've found a good place.

Inside, an old Mötley Crüe song says something about a rocket ship to outer space.

"This is it for you two," Sam says, still staring up. "You can go anywhere now."

"There's this story my dad tells," I say, "about three servants, and their boss gives them a bunch of money. Two of them invest their shares, and their boss is really happy when he comes home. The third buries it, and his boss is pissed."

"Dude," Lucas says eventually. "What does that have do with stars?"

"Sam said we could go anywhere. The story means we can't bury our gifts. We have to go out and take risks."

Sam begins vibrating beside me. After a minute, she breaks into giggles again.

"What?"

"You're the least risk-taking person I know," she says.

On my other side, Lucas begins vibrating, too.

"That's not true!"

"Oh my God, there's a pink heart on my locker, everyone's going to see it," Lucas says in falsetto.

"Shut up."

"I can't go to the party tonight. I have to help my grandpa brush his teeth," Sam says.

Soon they're both in hysterics. Every time they're close to regaining control, one of them pipes up again.

"You're the only seventeen-year-old in history who drives under the speed limit," Sam says.

Lucas has rolled onto his side. One hand pounds the ground.

"Your shirts, even your new ones, are all gray." Sam can barely manage words. "Did you know they were all gray?"

Okay, I hadn't realized this. Still...

"Just because I'm not some spotlight personality doesn't mean I can't take risks." I say "spotlight personality" with air quotes and a hefty dose of sarcasm, but Sam is immune at the moment.

"Hey, I jumped in the river that day!" Finally, I come up with proof.

"That was *highly* dangerous," Lucas agrees. Apparently, I'm not the only master of sarcasm.

"C'mon," Sam says, pulling herself up and tugging at Lucas and me. "Let's go back inside. Show me some dance floor risk-taking."

That almost sends both her and Lucas back to the ground, but they manage — barely — to hold it together until we're dancing again.

That's when Sam stiffens.

"Good fucking grief," she says in an entirely different tone of voice.

I follow her gaze to the door of the gym, where her dad stands scanning the crowd, looking wide and solid as an old-growth stump in his uniform and brush cut.

Lucas disappears into the gyrating mass. Sam grabs my hips and grinds against me, throwing her head back and whooping above the music. My sway becomes a stagger as I fight to keep my balance, hold her and keep an eye on her dad at the same time.

"What are you doing?" My words disappear into the bass.

Corporal Ko saunters toward a chaperoning teacher. He stops to ask a few questions at a table full of girls drinking punch that I'm sure is spiked. When he finds one kid half-cut with his forehead on a table, he beckons another chaperone over.

Sam puts a hand on my chin and draws my head close to hers. She kisses me. With tongue.

As soon as she stops, I glance back toward her dad. He's staring above our heads, over the sea of dancers.

"That's it. We're getting out of here," Sam says.

Which of course is what I've wanted to do since before we arrived. We slip out the side doors of the gym and make a run for it.

•

We're half a block from the school, walking between the far-apart streetlight circles, when Lucas catches up to us.

"Where are you guys going?"

I can still hear the sounds of the dance behind us.

"Just walking," I tell him.

"I'm done with grad," Lucas says. Then he stretches his arms into the sky. "Done with all of it. Done!"

"Let's do something crazy." Sam smiles up at us, waving her own jazz hands in the air and looking a little off-kilter. "You in?"

There's an especially wild spark in her eyes that I haven't seen before.

"Hell, yeah," Lucas says.

Where Canyon Street turns toward the highway, Summer Motors glows in neon blue and green. Helium balloons rise like multicolored UFOs from new and used cars. Sam hops the ditch into the lot and starts shopping.

"You'd buy this one," she tells Lucas, standing in front of a black pickup with chrome roll bars. "Opposites attract."

Lucas laughs.

"This one's yours," she calls to me over the roof of a cherry-red Corvette. She's trying the handles of every car she passes.

"If I were a pimp."

"Or a drug dealer," Lucas says.

I shoot him a quick glare, but he's checking out the mags on another sports car.

Suddenly, Sam squeals. "This one's mine!"

She's found an unlocked door. Already she's behind the wheel. It's a butt-ugly blue pickup with orange pulses painted down the sides. A remnant of the nineties.

The engine roars to life.

"What the hell?" Lucas says.

"Get in!"

"Duck!" Lucas says at the same time.

I drop automatically, the way I might when a helicopter passes overhead. Sam cuts the engine. From behind the truck, peering over the edge of the metal, I can see a police cruiser sliding by on the highway. It seems to slow as it passes the car lot. I hold my breath.

Then it's gone, and Sam is muttering curses as she turns the key again. Lucas slides in beside her and I follow, as if we're waterfowl and there's safety in squeezing together.

"What are you doing?" Lucas says.

Sam rolls down all the windows.

"Keys were in the ignition," she crows. "It was meant to be mine!"

Damn small towns and their lack of security measures.

She throws it in reverse, barely missing the Corvette behind her. Then she does her own NASCAR circuit of the lot. I have to admit, she drives well in tight confines. She might have a future in the sport.

She brakes at the edge of the highway and revs the engine.

14

If all your friends jumped off a cliff, would you? What if you assumed they were just going to stand at the edge of the cliff and enjoy the view?

Sam and Lucas laugh like maniacs.

"All right. Can we park this thing now?" I ask.

Sam yells, "Test drive! This is risk-taking, baby!"

She peels out of the lot and down Canyon Street toward town.

At first Lucas keeps laughing about the ass-whipping some sales guy will get tomorrow morning when the boss finds out the keys were left in this truck. We're all still running on the fumes of the pot and the booze, I suppose. I have to grip the dash to stay upright while Sam swerves into the opposing lane and passes a slow-moving car.

She pulls off Canyon Street to circle the high school, waving an arm out the window and yelling, "See you on the other side, suckers!"

A few stragglers holler back from outside the gym doors.

Only when Sam decides to reverse down the main drag

at full speed do I really start to panic. My foot pushes frantically on a phantom brake petal.

"Okay, I get your point. I'm not a risk-taker," I say through gritted teeth.

But this isn't about risk-taking. Looking at her face, I can see that. Her jaw is set in grim determination now.

It's like she wants to be caught.

How did I not see this before I climbed in? She's going to get her dad's attention tonight — and ruin her potential policing career — through any means possible. Corporal Ko won't be able to gaze at the wall above her head once we've all been busted.

Sam throws the truck into Drive, tears through town a third time, blows a red light in front of Burger Barn, and skids onto 25th.

Lucas seems frozen in place, his smile still plastered across his cheeks but his eyes wide.

As Sam takes another corner so fast that the back tilts and slides behind us, I tell her to stop. To slow down. To pull over.

"You can talk to your dad a different way!"

"Screw that." Cranking the classic rock station, the one that's been playing since she turned the key, she heads downhill. It's as if Lucas and I are debris swept along in a mudslide.

When I yell at her again, she starts singing along to the radio.

"You're trying to get caught," I shout. "That's not risk-taking. That's just stupid."

For a brief moment, when the siren wails behind us, it seems imaginary, as if we're in a movie scene and of course this is what happens next. But even as I'm thinking that, I'm also flipping through possible consequences.

This is no movie. This is my entire family about to pay for the bad decisions I made tonight.

She speeds up.

"Sam!"

She burns along another residential street, takes the corner hard and floors the pedal.

"It's a high-speed chase. Don't worry, they're not supposed to keep coming. They might endanger civilians." She leans over the steering wheel, focused on the road. We take another corner, fast enough that Lucas loses his grip on the dash and crushes me against the door.

The cops apparently don't interpret the rules the same way Sam does. They're still coming. The interior of the truck flashes red, then blue.

Yelling isn't helping. I shove Lucas off me.

"Sam, maybe your dad can get you out of this, but mine can't." I'm still yelling. She's still staring straight ahead. I flick the music off and force myself to lower my voice. "We need to stop."

But what good is that going to do? Getting arrested isn't an option.

Another patrol car joins the first. The siren volume doubles. Sam turns the music back on.

"Okay," Lucas shouts. He seems to have regained mental control. "I have a plan. Sam, after the next corner, you brake fast. We all dive out, and we run. If they can't catch us, they'll have no proof we were here."

She whips around the next corner. She fails to stop.

"Sam, I can't get arrested." I lean across Lucas to grab her arm. "Not just for normal reasons. It's different for me.

If you and I care about each other at all, I need to get out of this truck."

Her eyes shift toward me, then back to the road. On the steering wheel, her hands are like claws.

"Sam?"

My head bashes Lucas's chest when she hits the gas again.

"What the hell?"

Then she squeals to a stop. "Go! Now!"

Before my brain has rebounded, I yank open the door and sprint across a stranger's lawn. When I look back, I see Lucas streaking in the opposite direction. The siren seems deafening and the lights like strobes as the cop cars round the corner. An officer leaps from the first car and races after Lucas.

Just as the second patrol car pulls in behind her truck, Sam roars away from the curb.

She didn't run.

I scramble up a backyard fence and down the other side, narrowly missing a wagon and a trike. Then I'm across yet another fence and through a garden, and out the space between houses on the other side.

Why didn't she run?

I know the answer before I finish forming the question.

All of this — the car chase, the bump and grind, the mixed booze — it was all about getting caught.

I have to lean on my knees for a second to catch my breath as another thought strikes me. Maybe our whole relationship was about getting caught. Why else would a girl like Sam date a shitrat like me?

There are no lights on in the house, or in the neighboring houses. There's only the glow of the streetlight from the end of the block and the faraway fading siren.

No one's followed me. Maybe there was only one cop in that car and he chose to chase Sam. Maybe he rounded the corner too late to see me. Maybe God's watching over me.

My lungs feel as if I've seared the lining from them.

Slowly, I walk to the end of the block and figure out where I am, approximately. Then I start toward the south side of town. Toward the orchard.

•

It's a long walk, dark and silent. I have plenty of time to recognize what a mess I've made.

In the past month, I've turned my entire life into one of Big Bugger's shit piles. I've disappointed Dad, blown my chance at art school and discovered my girlfriend is a lunatic. Possibly a lying lunatic.

I'm every word that Walt has ever thrown at me.

Part of me — a big part — wants to crawl into the ditch alongside the orchard and stay there. Because there's no way to fix this. The only solution I can think of is to leave, immediately, for the grow. Stay close to the cabin until I'm sure all of this has blown over. Possibly until Sam's dad is transferred to another detachment.

That could be years. I'll be working on the grow for years.

I feel as if I've swallowed a pine cone and it's lodged in my throat. But I can't see any other option.

When I reach Judith's place, sweaty and exhausted, it's Garrett who answers the door. Turquoise briefs and a surprisingly furry chest.

"I think you'd better sleep it off somewhere and come back in the morning," he says.

"Sweetheart?" Judith's voice calls from the dark. She's made it back from the mountain, obviously.

"I need to talk to her," I say, my breath still ragged.

"Are you high?" he asks.

That's not an excuse.

He leans against the doorframe as if he owns the place, but that's not a good excuse, either.

I really have no excuse for what I do next.

I haul him out, drag him over the plastic step and press him against the metal side of the bus. I'm so angry that I barely know what I'm doing, yet somehow I have time to be surprised that I'm this much bigger and stronger than Judith's weasel.

It feels good to grind my forearms into his chest.

"What the hell?" When Judith pokes her bed head outside, Garrett has both arms in the air, surrendering to a crazy person.

"I need help," I tell her.

"This is an interesting way to ask for it."

I love my sister. Nothing riles her.

"I tried other ways."

She's already gone back inside. I hear her rummaging around, presumably getting dressed. Slowly, I loosen my grip on Garrett.

"Fuck, man," he says, rubbing his neck.

I don't feel like apologizing. Instead I walk to Judith's car and shift from foot to foot beside the door, waiting for her to emerge.

Garrett, after glaring at me for a few more minutes, bangs his way back into the bus.

"No way you're going with him." I hear his voice through the thin walls, as clearly as if he were standing beside me.

"He's my brother, baby."

Since when does Judith call anyone "baby"?

"Fuck that. He's high as a kite, and whatever trouble he's in, it's not your problem." The wall shudders with the smack of his hand. I take a step toward the door.

But then…

"I have to go. I'll make it up to you." Judith emerges, hopping down the stairs and over the grass toward me. And if I loved her before, I love her double now for the way she leaves everything she has, without a moment's hesitation, because I need her.

•

I sit in the silence of Judith's car in the middle of the police parking lot, shivering. A big part of me wants to push through the glass doors and demand to know where Lucas and Sam are, what's going on, what's taking so long. They must both be in there. If they had gotten away, Judith would be back by now.

I press my fingers into my forehead, trying to squeeze out all the stupid things I've done tonight.

There's a moth beside me, perfectly still on a brown blanket that Judith has thrown over her console. He's like a visitor from home. I lean closer. It's shocking how perfect something so tiny can be. He has double wings — the outer ones speckled brown on brown and the inner ones in a minuscule pattern of waves. On his head there are antennae thinner than the hairs on my arm.

I wonder what he keeps in that pin-sized brain. Does he know only want? Need? Does a moth have dreams? Is he purely survival instinct, or does he make choices?

I move my hand closer, wanting to brush my finger along the edge of his perfect wing, but I startle him and he's up, flapping and zigzagging like an out-of-control fighter pilot.

I crack open the door and he darts at the car's overhead light. That's a choice made in the pressure of a moment that's obviously not the right one. Which only leaves the question of whether my brain is better equipped than a moth's.

I scoop him toward the door and finally he's outside. He can fly all the way back up the mountain if his little wings can carry him that far. But they don't. Even as I watch, he's distracted by the light beside the police station door. He flaps in erratic circles around the bulb.

I'm about to draw final conclusions on my own life, when the door swings open and Judith emerges, Lucas in tow.

"I couldn't get Sam," Judith says as she climbs into the driver's side. "She's with her dad."

Lucas folds himself into the back seat. His teeth are chattering. There's something heartbreaking about a big guy with chattering teeth. I throw him the moth's blanket.

"Sorry," he says.

"What are you sorry for? We both climbed into that truck."

He shrugs. His eyes look shiny in the dark.

"Let's blow this pop stand." Judith is actually grinning as she starts the car. Lucas gives her directions to his house.

"Did they call your dad?" I ask Lucas, turning back to peer at him again.

Lucas nods for a minute, then shakes his head. The guy is obviously traumatized.

"Really?"

He shrugs. "Judith said my parents were out of town. Said she was my cousin."

"It's all in the eyelashes," Judith says.

"She's good in a crisis," I say. My sister just walked straight into a police station for me — something that must have gone against every ounce of her upbringing. I look at her with a new admiration. "That was heroic, breaking this guy out."

"Sam must have told them I wasn't driving," Lucas says.

"Did you see her? Before you left?"

They both shake their heads.

I shouldn't see her, either. I should walk away. After watching her drive that truck, every moment of our past few weeks seems skewed. When we were in the hot tub, was she hoping we'd get caught? Did she ask me to pick her up for breakfast knowing her dad would be home, and knowing he'd call me a shitrat? How many times did she mention me just to see if he'd take the bait?

The questions make my gut clench.

Yet I still want to see her. I suppose I want to look in her eyes and know if the worst is true.

Judith pulls up to the curb outside Lucas's house.

"Text me later," I tell him.

He gives me a twisted sort of smile, like he's in pain.

Judith takes me to her place after that. It's thankfully free of Garrett, though not of the stench of Garrett's cologne.

"Hey," I say, before we fall asleep. "Thanks."

"Anytime," she says.

•

I stare into blackness for the rest of the night, until birds start chirping in the orchard trees.

Gradually the silhouettes of kitchen cupboards take shape above me.

It's finally morning.

Judith snores softly, a pillow half over her head.

When I climb to my feet, my knees are wobbly. My eyes feel as if someone's poured acid into them. My head aches. But mostly I feel weighted down. There's a mix of sad and angry churning around in my gut.

I feel terrible about Lucas. I hope his dad was asleep when we dropped him off last night.

But it's more than that. I'm mad at myself for leaving the cabin yesterday and going to the grad ceremony. I'm even more angry that I climbed into that pickup. And I'm furious at Sam for intentionally landing us in trouble. She barreled straight toward disaster and dragged Lucas and me along with her.

Judith hasn't stirred. As quietly as possible in a place that shakes when I breathe, I pull on my crumpled suit pants, tuck my jacket and my art book into a bundle under my arm and let myself out.

The cool air feels like a slap, in a good way. I take a few gulps, then start to walk, heading for the school parking lot and my truck.

•

I park down the street from Sam's house and text her. Then I wait. I must doze off, eventually, because my phone startles me when it buzzes.

Sam's home. She's going to sneak out and meet me at the playground down the street.

When she arrives, I'm standing in the trees at the far edge of the park, half-hidden in the shade. I wave, and she joins me. She's dressed in the most conventional outfit I've ever seen her wear: jeans and a black T-shirt. She looks like a twelve-year-old kid.

"Hey." She doesn't meet my eyes.

Somehow, I thought she'd apologize.

"You okay?"

She nods.

"That was scary," I say, careful to keep my voice level. "What the hell, Sam?"

She kicks at the gravel with the toe of her sneaker.

"I guess I want to know if you had it all planned. This whole spring, was I supposed to be bait? A shitrat to drive your dad nuts?"

She winces then and mumbles something.

"What?"

"Side benefit."

I feel as if I could reach back and rip out one of these trees.

"So you were using me." A picture flashes into my head of her holding a huckleberry blossom in her hand. It was all fake.

"I wasn't using you!" Her voice cracks. "I liked you. You were different. And you could do anything you wanted, if you didn't have your head up your ass."

"What does that even mean?"

"Maybe you're the one who was using me!"

"For what? How would I be using you?" I'm yelling now, but there's a voice inside my head telling me she's right. What was my entire "temporary leave of absence" plan, if it didn't include her?

I grit my teeth. "I'm not the one with the spotlight personality, looking for attention all the time. Did it work? Are you happy now?"

"Yeah. I'm fucking ecstatic, Zac. Can't you tell?"

Walt would really love this girl.

"I don't think we can see each other anymore."

She laughs, an angry, bitter laugh that doesn't match at all with her new makeup-free face. "Thanks for clarifying."

So I leave. I hear chains rattle behind me, and when I glance back, she's sitting on one of the swings, watching me. She doesn't look angry anymore. She looks...guilty.

I set my jaw and force myself to climb into the truck, close the door and drive away.

•

When I cut the engine on the ATV, in that moment before the birds start singing again, there's a perfect stillness. I want to burrow inside it the way I used to dive into piles of leaves when I was small.

A crow is the first, his loud caw echoing through the trees. A squirrel natters at me from high above. As my ears adjust, I hear small rustlings and brushings. Fur against branch, leaf against leaf.

I make my way up the trail, feeling the town fade behind me. Oil and gas replaced by the thick, dusky smell of the woods. A faint rumble below as a big truck passes on the highway, then nothing but wind again, rattling branches.

It's entirely peaceful here, yet I feel as if I've been mauled by wild animals and left to die.

At the crunch of a branch, I look uphill.

It's Hazel. She's snuffling her big cinnamon-brown snout in welcome. I drop to my butt in the middle of the trail, wait for her to plod toward me, then wrap my arms around her massive neck and press my forehead into her shoulder. My chest cracks open and suddenly my whole body's shaking.

Hazel lets out a long, slow sigh and butts my head gently with hers.

"You should be happy," I tell her, once I regain some control. "You have no competition now."

15

I throw myself into work, adding hours of chores onto the daily watering. At first I split cedar into kindling. Dad has a mallet and an L-shaped tool called a froe. It's strangely satisfying to bang the froe into the wood and split the cedar along the grain. Sheets of it pile up around me. But after a while, it's too repetitive. There's a rhythm to the work and my hands begin to operate automatically, leaving me too much time to think. Too much time to remember Sam's lips, or the arc of her eyebrow.

I switch to painting the cabin logs. Dad bought stain a few years ago, but he never got around to using it. The half-rusted cans are stacked in the shadow of the drying shed. I pry the lid from the first one, dig up an old brush and go to work.

It takes me three days, half of that time balanced on a homemade ladder. I try to focus on the line between the old wood and the shiny stained version, the signs of progress, the constant up and down the ladder, back and forth along the beams.

But I can't stay focused all the time. I find myself picturing Sam's swing on the rope into the river. Or the way she dips both ends of each French fry in ketchup.

When Big Bugger knocks over my paint tray and plods off, leaving cedar-stain paw prints, I immediately imagine telling the story to Sam.

Then I remember we're not together and I could never tell her stories about bears, anyway. My insides echo like the blackened center of a lightning-struck tree.

Whenever Dad walks by, I try to gather the courage to tell him.

This is what I need to say: I've broken up with Sam, and my art school option didn't work out, but staying here is going to crush me.

•

Mom sees footprints while she's picking dandelion leaves near the logging road early one morning. She says there might have been fresh tire tracks on the road — it was hard to tell.

"Gotta move," Walt says. "Fucking prick."

"Probably nothing. Hikers," Dad says.

Which seems entirely unlike Dad. And how would hikers get a vehicle past the gate?

I follow Mom to a huckleberry patch after breakfast. There are still beads of moisture clinging to the leaves, and my legs are both slick and sliced by the time we've picked our way there. Big Bugger and Queenie have beaten us to it, but they're in a sugar stupor and barely glance in our direction. Hazel, on the other hand, would rather eat berries from my bucket than from the bushes.

"Don't be so lazy," I say, pushing her head away.

Mom efficiently pops the big orbs from their branches. They're dark blue-purple — almost black, plump and wide like blueberries on steroids. Soon our hands are stained with berry juice. When I look over at Mom, she has a purple streak on her chin.

"You're supposed to pick them, not eat them."

She tosses a berry at my head.

With her hair swinging in a ponytail, she could still be the teenager who met Dad at the counter of Sunset Seed Supply. She could still be the young mom who used to chase me through the woods. Or the mom who quizzed me on my times tables while balanced on a tree branch, because I'd refused to do my schoolwork inside that day.

"What?" she asks now.

I realize I've stopped picking. I've been staring at her.

"What do you think about Walt's other property? Does it exist?"

"Oh, it exists," she says. "This grow makes good money. He's probably got a few properties stashed away."

I let this sink in.

"So…do you think it's possible? To get Walt there and get set up again?" I ask finally.

"We'd manage. He says there's a cabin of some sort."

She's willing to risk the unknown. I suppose it's the same thing she did when she left town and followed Dad to their first grow. Then followed him to this property a few years later. Maybe the real risk-taker in my family is my herb-picking, tea-making mother.

"Do you think it's time to go?" I ask her.

"We left the old place without nearly so many signs of trouble."

"Laws have changed since then," I say.

"Not enough."

"So why isn't he packing?" Because it's Dad who seems stuck here like an old rootball.

"Lots of reasons," she says.

I stare at her until she elaborates.

"You. Judith. The bears."

"Judith and I can take care of ourselves."

But the bears. As I think about them, I see the problems. We can't load them into the pickup and drive them through town on our way to some other plot. They're habituated.

"We can't leave the bears behind, can we?"

"They'll go looking for food at the campground, or they'll turn up at someone's lake house," she says. "And bears are territorial. If we managed to take them, they'd cause trouble at the new place."

Hazel chooses that moment to push her head beneath my arm, almost upsetting the berry bucket.

"You're a problem," I tell her, scratching behind her ear the way she likes.

A big problem. To leave the grow, Dad will have to abandon the bears. And though he doesn't know it, he'll have to go without me. It seems like a rough one-two punch to lay on a guy.

I look back at Mom, who's still eating as many berries as she's picking.

"If I ever left, I'd miss your huckleberry pancakes."

The words slip out. When I realize what I've said, I glance at her quickly.

She stares back at me, her hands stilled.

"Oh," she says. She turns her head away slightly, but I can still see her eyelashes blinking fast.

I wait. I want to reach for her, to touch her arm. I want to make everything okay. But it doesn't seem possible to make everything okay for everyone.

"Well, it's a big world out there," she says finally.

I don't know whether that's a warning or a blessing.

•

Within a few more days, I'm going crazy. I've split enough kindling to last us a year. The cabin's stained. I've greased each of Dad's traps. I even extracted a mangled squirrel from one and tossed it to the nearest bear. I've checked each water line and hose for leaks and replaced a rusty connection.

I have to talk to him.

Mom keeps tearing up when she's around me. Dad must realize that something's changed. Even Walt seems to know. They all watch me the way I watch Big Bugger.

Finally, Mom sits down across from me while Dad's out feeding the animals one morning.

"I found your email from the art school."

"Mom!"

"I did the laundry. It was in your back pocket."

Walt grunts from his chair. When I glance over, he's holding my book of paintings. The book Sam made.

"What the hell?" I hiss.

Mom shrugs. "He wanted to see it. And I think we should talk about — "

"George," Walt says, squinting at me. "George...Ib. Ib."

I have no idea what he's trying to say. Maybe he's forgotten my name. I cross the room in two strides, pull the book and the paper from under his hand and head for the lean-to.

"Not...name..."

I don't wait to hear the rest of his gibberish. As soon as my stuff is safely tucked beneath my mattress, I stomp out of the house and slam the door.

I'm done with having everyone in my shit. I'm going to do it today. I'll arrange things with Judith, then I'll talk to Dad. No more chickening out.

•

When I pull down the drive, Judith's sitting in her lawn chair. She goes inside before I park and closes the door after herself.

I don't think too much about it. I figure she needs to put on her bra or brush her teeth. Mostly I'm just glad Garrett's car isn't here. I'm definitely not ready to discuss future plans in front of that guy. I can't even say his name without my lip curling.

I tap on the door.

She doesn't answer, so I flop into a lawn chair to wait.

I wait a long time.

"Hey, Judith!" I tip my chair back so I can knock on the side of the bus. "Any chance of breakfast?"

There's a long silence.

"Today's not good," she says finally, her voice muffled.

What's that supposed to mean?

"We can go out. I have cash. I need to talk to you."

"I've got stuff to do."

What the...

Now I know something's wrong. I get up from the chair and stare at the bus, as if the walls might suddenly turn transparent. Which they don't.

"I'm not leaving," I call.

Silence.

"What's going on?"

Silence.

"I'm counting to three, and if you're not out here, I'm breaking down your door."

How exactly do they break doors in the movies? I feel as if I should run and ram my shoulder against it, but Judith's entrance is raised a few steps. I'd have to jump. Plus, her door opens out. Maybe if I braced one leg against the metal frame and hauled on it?

I shrug. This entire ancient bus is a piece of crap. If worst comes to worst, I can flip it on its side and shake it.

"One..."

"Two..."

Thank God. Before I get to three and have to maim myself, she opens the door. She doesn't come out, though. She just lets the door swing free.

I step up and peer in, as if I might be entering Big Bugger's den. There are no lights on and the curtains are drawn, but once my eyes adjust, I spot her sitting at the table. Her hair hangs limp, covering half her face.

"You all right?"

"Just a rough night," she says. "Make yourself some toast."

I pull out a loaf of bread and pop a few slices into the toaster oven. Her coffee maker's still half-full, so I pour myself a giant cup. Then I slide onto the bench across from my sister.

She doesn't look up.

"You going to tell me what's going on?"

"Just stuff," she says. "Private stuff." She raises her own mug to her lips.

In that moment, as she tips her chin to drink, I see the shadow on her face. I reach across and lift her hair away. She bats at my hand, but not quickly enough.

Her eye is swollen, barely open, and a nasty mix of purple and black.

"What the hell happened?" I sound half like Dad and half like Walt, which is not what I intend. But there's something about seeing my sister like this. My whole body's suddenly tight and pulsing.

"Drunk guy at work," Judith says.

"I'll kill him."

"Don't be ridiculous," she says.

My toast pops.

"I'm not being ridiculous. You tell me who it was right now."

She gets up to butter the toast. I don't think it's just her eye. She's moving like an eighty-year-old woman.

I get up, too, mostly because I can't stay still anymore. But before I can figure out my next step, a car roars up the drive.

Garrett.

"Fuck," Judith breathes. She puts down the butter knife and holds the counter with both hands, head dropped.

I move to the doorframe. I lean against one side and brace my arm against the other, like a human barricade.

"Hey, kid," Garrett says as he climbs from his car. "Your sister around?"

He walks toward me. "I gotta talk to her before work."

I glance at Judith, who is still gripping the counter. She shakes her head slightly.

I'm still not a hundred percent sure. That's what holds me in the doorway. She could be hiding from him the same way she hid from me. It could be true, what she said. It could have been a drunk guy at the bar.

Garrett has both hands in the air now, like a man surrendering.

"Listen, I had too much to drink last night. I know things went a little crazy. But if I talk to her — "

Before he can finish, I hurl myself from the bus and knock him flat on his back. I have tunnel vision. Black-and-white static everywhere, with only a tiny clear circle in the center. A circle just big enough for his face.

He tries to push me off him, but there's no way. I pound through his arm blocks. I slam a fist into his jaw. Then another. He shoves me off-balance and my next swing hits his nose. There's a satisfying crunch. Blood smears across his cheek.

I've heard nothing until now except the roar in my head, but Judith has her fingernails in my shoulders and she's pulling. She screams in my ear.

"Stop! Stop it!"

A big part of me — the part with my fist already raised again — wants to keep pounding Garrett until he's spattered into the dirt. But when Judith grabs my arm and clings, I let her stop me.

As I shift my weight off him, Garrett rolls to his side, hands covering his face.

"This is assault," he says, his voice barely intelligible.

"Are you fucking serious?" I'm not intelligible either. It's more of a snarl than speech. "I'm going to count to three, and you're going to get in your car and drive away and you'd better never, ever show your face here again..."

I'm big on counting this morning, apparently.

"One…two…"

He staggers to his feet, blood dripping onto his shirt. He doesn't make it to the car in time, but he's trying, so I hold onto the "three" until he's gone.

Once he drives away, my adrenaline leaks away. I drop to the grass, where I lie on my back and look up at Judith. She looks a decade older than she should.

"Why'd you lie?"

"I didn't lie, exactly. He was at the bar last night, drunk, and he didn't like the way I was acting with the other customers."

"You could have told me that."

"I didn't want you to kill him."

"I didn't kill him," I say, raising an arm off the ground to examine my fist. I open and close the fingers. Bruised, but otherwise fine. I don't think I've ever hit anyone before.

"Proud of yourself?" Judith asks, shaking her head. She eases to the grass beside me. In the sunlight, her eye looks even worse.

"I am, sort of," I grin. "Do you think being able to fight is genetic?"

She smirks. "If it is, you're probably the best rifle-shot in town."

I *am* a pretty decent shot.

"Ironically, Walt started the grow because he didn't want to fight."

"Or maybe he didn't want to follow orders," Judith says. "Can you imagine?"

"Fucking prick," I say in Walt's voice.

She cups a hand over her eye. "Ouch. Don't make me laugh."

"What now?" I ask.

"What about what now?" she says.

"He might come back."

She shrugs. "I'll call the cops. I can do that, you know. I'm not the one growing pot."

Suddenly she's crying, looking away from me and across the orchard.

"Hey." I slide over on the grass until I can put an arm around her. "It's done now. He's gone."

"It's not even that," she says. "It's just...this is harder than I thought it would be, you know? It's lonely. I get paid crap."

"What about your courses?"

"What am I going to do with a psychology degree? Besides, it'll take years at the rate I'm going."

"Do you want to come home for a while?"

I almost laugh. I came to tell her I was leaving the grow, and now I'm encouraging her to go back.

"You could give this some time to blow over, then think about starting again."

"Can you leave twice?" She looks at me as if I might really know the answer. But I don't.

I make her breakfast. Then I leave for a while, drop off a lawyer envelope for Walt and hit the hardware store for rope and duct tape. I stop by her place again on the way home and offer to stay the night.

Judith shakes her head.

"He won't come back tonight," she says.

"I could stay to keep you company."

"No," she says. "I gotta deal with it eventually."

Which is exactly how I feel as I pull my truck onto the highway.

16

Hazel meets me as I crest the hill, but I slip into the drying shed, push her nose out of the way and close the door behind me. I suppose I'm looking for one last moment of peace before all hell breaks loose.

I reach for Dad's stash, tucked above the frame of the one small window, and I roll myself a different kind of temporary absence. Then I lower myself to the slat floor and wrap my arms around my knees.

After a while, the scenes on the walls begin to look more real than ever. They must have taken months to draw. Years. The faces of the people in the San Francisco street scene are incredibly detailed. I can even see the relationships between them. An old woman leans on the arm of a younger girl. A toddler runs through the crowd holding a stuffed lion against his chest, mouth wide in laughter. A harried-looking mother chases behind. There's a young couple in a restaurant window holding hands across the table. The man is partly obscured, but the woman's face is clear.

She has Walt's eyes.

These could all be real people. Maybe Walt populated

his mural with figures from his past. This girl…his sister, maybe? She looks like she's in her early twenties, a little younger than Walt would have been when he was drafted.

I never thought to wonder about the family Walt left. He's always seemed like the trunk of our family tree. But of course he's a branch like the rest of us. When he deserted from Vietnam, then crossed the border to Canada, he left people behind.

I know my dad will never understand why anyone would want to leave these woods. But Walt…maybe Walt will get it. He had to give up both his family and his art when he chose to live here. Or at least the possibility of sharing his art. Sharing his worldview, as Mr. Pires might say.

I suck in one last lungful, probably sacrificing a few brain cells for the sake of courage.

I'll never be a spotlight personality. I know that. But I can't put all my art into a shed, either.

Inside the cabin, I find Mom, Dad and Walt sitting around the table. They look as though they may have been arguing, but I don't let that stop me. I drop into the chair across from Dad.

"I'm going to move to town for a while." This is the only way I know how to say it. I have to blurt the words. "I'll stay with Judith while I look for work. Then I'm going to save up and apply to art school next year."

Silence. My eyes skitter their way to the cabin wall above their heads, and it takes all my willpower to drag my gaze back to Dad.

He looks heartbroken. As if his face is caving in on itself. But as I watch, he hardens.

"Well, that's fine," he says.

A brief flare of hope —

"Do whatever you damn well please."

When I glance at Mom, her cheeks are wet. Walt, for once, is silent.

"I know it's a bad time," I say.

Dad pushes himself up from the table and heads for the door.

"Do what you gotta do," he says.

Communication. We really lost the genetic lottery on that one.

•

Once Dad disappears, I can't stand the way Walt keeps muttering about someone named George. I can't handle the sadness leaking from Mom. I throw my stuff into my pack and promise that I'll check in within the next few days.

Hazel joins me as soon as I walk out the door. She follows me down the trail, past the ATV and toward the logging road. For a while she scouts ahead. Then she stops to nose a dead tree and I pass her. But she doesn't like that, and a few minutes later she bounds by me. Which feels a bit like being passed by a dump truck on a single-lane road.

"It's a good thing I love you," I say.

I'm not ready to leave her. I toss my pack in the back of the truck on my way past, then I lead the way to the highway. Hazel doesn't stop until we're a few steps from the ditch that marks our side, a bit north of the campground. There, she waits for me to catch up.

It's almost dusk. A lone pickup drives by, then nothing.

I hop across the ditch, listen carefully for any wandering druids, and give Hazel a wave.

"C'mon."

She does her own surprisingly agile leap over the bank and crosses the highway as if she owns it.

On the other side of the pavement there's a gradual bank just high enough to hide us from the road. Then a tiny crescent of beach. There's not a lot of room here, or sand, but there's enough space for me to settle on the pebbles and lean back against a log, and enough space for Hazel to drop onto her haunches beside me.

The lake is a perfect mirror. Upside-down mountains and blue sky and the tiniest brush of a cloud. For a few minutes, all I can hear are soft ripples.

This is probably my favorite place in the whole world.

"That your bear?"

The voice makes me scramble to my feet. Hazel, too. She sniffs at the air, assessing.

The man sidesteps in flip-flops down the bank from the highway. He's scruffy, unshaven and carrying a too-big backpack with a water bottle and a pair of hiking shoes tied to the side.

I glance at Hazel, then back at him.

There's no way to pretend she isn't tame. No way to pretend she's not with me.

"I wouldn't call her my bear, but we've known each other a long time. Her mother was killed by a hunter."

"Safe to sit down?" he asks, nodding at the log beside me.

When I shrug, he drops his pack and swings his leg over, placing himself on my left, leaving plenty of room between himself and the bear.

"You live here?"

"Nearby." I sit cautiously, examining him from the corner of my eye. He asks a lot of questions for a stranger.

"Just asked 'cause I could use a shower. It's taken me three days to get here from Vancouver, hitching. I'm heading to Fernie. Got friends there."

He gives a lot of information for a stranger, too. But his smile is friendly. Too friendly?

"Don't have a shower you can use, sorry. Might have a snack." I rummage in my pack and pull out a granola bar from the bottom. "It's probably been in there a while."

He doesn't care, apparently. He rips open the wrapper.

I figure he'll move on when he's done. But he settles in beside us.

It's time to get Hazel away.

I stand and brush the sand from my ass.

"We should get going. Good luck with your trip."

He nods again. "Nice to meet you."

He waits on the beach and watches as Hazel and I climb to the highway, check for traffic, cross the road and jump the ditch.

He watches, and I don't like it.

"Go home," I tell Hazel firmly, as soon as we're in the shadow of the trees. "Git. Go home." I give her a slap on the rump for emphasis, but she doesn't need it. Maybe she hears the tension in my voice. She lumbers up the old road without looking back. Partway along, she plows into the trees.

When I glance at the road, the stranger's standing on the shoulder, staring up toward our property. A car passes, but he doesn't put his thumb out. Instead, he turns and saunters north.

Which is not the direction of Fernie.

I keep watching.

A few minutes later, an old white Dodge drives by, and I spot the stranger's face in the passenger seat.

In the driver's seat, a familiar-looking brush cut.

I feel as if they've run me over with that car. My pulse thunders in my chest and in my head. My ears ring so loudly that I can hardly hear the nattering squirrel above me. I try to start hiking up the trail, but I can't catch my breath. I have to stop and put my hands on my knees.

They've probably been gathering evidence all week.

I'm an idiot. I've destroyed my entire family. For a girl who wasn't worth it.

How do I explain this to Dad?

Sam told. I remember these same words echoing in my head after she blabbed to her friends about Hazel. And if she couldn't keep that secret, what made me think she could ever be trusted? She knew I lived in the woods, had access to pot, didn't like cops. Of course she told her dad. I'm the shitrat who'll force Corporal Ko to pay attention, shine a big fucking spotlight on Sam's life. And mine.

I force my feet to move. One step after another.

We'll have no choice but to relocate.

Then I think of Hazel. I have to tell Hazel, is what I think, which makes no actual sense. But it's enough to make me wonder if I might have a stroke right here in the trees.

Which wouldn't necessarily be a bad thing. Because then I wouldn't have to deal with the fallout from any of this.

"Fucking prick," I mutter.

I have only myself to swear at.

•

Hazel meets me halfway up and I navigate the last part of the trail by keeping one hand on her rear. It's pitch black by the time I reach the cabin

When I push open the door, I startle them all.

There's an insistent knot in my gut.

"I ran into a hitchhiker by the highway."

Dad's eyes narrow.

"And?" he asks.

We just had our biggest fight ever, but he trusts my judgment. With that one word, he's relying on me to make the call.

"We have a problem."

"Fucking prick," Walt says.

"Yeah. That's what I thought, too."

Dad leans back in his chair. His breath comes out in a long, slow sigh. Then he clunks the chair legs down and raps his fist against the table.

"Fine. We leave first thing in the morning."

"This is my fault," I burst out. "I think Sam might have said something."

The look Dad gives me is like a fork to the gut. I deserve it, too. That's what makes this a million times worse. Over the past couple of months, I've broken every rule he ever taught me.

"I'm so sorry," I say.

He shakes his head. "Let's get this done."

Leaving Mom to pack the cabin, we take a couple of flashlights outside to gather the equipment. The generator has to stay, obviously, but the water pump can come. Some folded camo netting, a few coils of rope and a pared-down toolkit — heavy as hell but necessary.

"How will Walt get down the trail?" I ask Dad when we cross paths.

He smirks. "The old coot's been practicing laps of the cabin for weeks. He knew."

I add a tarp for shelter, in case Walt's cabin on the new lot proves imaginary.

It's past midnight by the time we're finished. Inside, Mom has reduced our essentials to one large pack. It almost looks as if nothing's changed. The rifles are leaning by the door, ready to go. The blanket's missing from the back of Walt's chair. I'm sure if I checked the cupboards, I'd find a pot and some food gone. But that's it. My lean-to looks almost exactly the same as always.

We're probably the only family in the world that packs camouflage netting instead of clean underwear.

Shaking my head, I collapse onto my bed. I fall asleep to the chant of *fucking prick, fucking prick* in my brain.

•

Dad wakes me at dawn. I don't know if he slept. He might have kept watch from the front stoop all night, the bears gathered like sentries around him.

Mom sets bowls of oatmeal on the table.

"Bears go," Walt says once we're finished. He pushes himself up.

Dad and I look at each other. Neither one of us wants to admit that Walt's right.

"Maybe...a zoo...." But I've already run through these possibilities in my head. The bears are habituated, so no animal rescue place will take them. And how would I get five bears to a zoo? There isn't a zoo anywhere near here and even if there were, there would be regulations and paperwork. I'd have to explain how I came by five semi-tame beasts.

It would be terrible to leave them in cages anyway. Like locking them all in the drying shed.

"Bears," Walt says again. He's already holding the Winchester.

Dad stands suddenly, knocking his chair over behind him. He draws a breath and it feels like the tremor before a volcano erupts.

The cabin door bangs open.

Between Mom, Dad, Walt and me, I think there's almost a quadruple heart attack.

We're too late.

That's my first thought. Before I've even formulated it, Walt has raised his rifle.

"Fuck that," Judith says. "Don't start shooting again."

My sister, sweat plastering her hair to her neck, drops a small pack by the door. Her bruise has faded slightly, to a puffy blue-green.

"You guys know there's a ghost car at the bottom of the logging road? I had to park in the campground."

"Fucking prick," Walt says.

"Nice to see you, too," she says.

There's something in the cocky set of her shoulders when she says it that almost makes me smile. Doesn't seem like Judith will be taking any shit.

"So are we going?" she asks.

When neither Dad nor I answer, Mom says, "Isaac has chosen to stay behind."

As if that's the most important thing right now.

"Welcome home, sis," I say.

"You're leaving?" She raises her eyebrows. Is it possible she looks impressed?

"I'll help with the move first. And we need to figure out what to do with the bears."

"We're not taking the damn bears," she says.

She's going to get along well with Walt, this new version of my sister.

"Get it done, then," Dad says. His voice is thick as he turns away.

Walt's left me the Springfield. Mom hands me a slab of meat.

Outside, I whistle for them. Then I sling the haunch of venison into the space between the cabin and the outhouse. It doesn't take long for the bears to gather. I fit the butt of the rifle against my shoulder. I may not remember Walt teaching me to draw, but I remember him teaching me to shoot.

"You take the two to the right," I tell him.

The first shots shake my brain and set off a high-pitched whine in my ears. The Springfield has a killer recoil. It almost rips my shoulder off. But I drop one of the twins. Walt hits Queenie square in the chest. Then all hell breaks loose. The other twin and Hazel run bawling for the trees. Big Bugger roars — a thunderous roar like I've never heard. I swear the ground shakes. When he rears onto his hind legs, he's the height of the cabin.

My whole body quivers. I fire and miss.

Walt hits Big Bugger in the shoulder, then again in the chest. The bear drops to all fours, but he doesn't fall. He rushes us. He's not anyone's pet now. He barrels like a tank, closing the gap by half, three-quarters.

I can't hear anything. My fingers won't work. My vision has narrowed to a tunnel, which is entirely filled with six hundred pounds of rippling fur.

I manage to fire, finally.

My rifle's meant for long-range shooting. The round hits like a grenade and Big Bugger drops in a heap, almost at our feet.

"Fucking prick," Walt breathes.

I have to wait for my legs to stop shaking, but it takes me only one shot to drop the second twin from its tree.

There's only Hazel left. She's shimmied up a tree too small for her, and it's bowing back toward the ground while she hugs the trunk like a security blanket. She's practically at eye level. When I walk over, she turns her head to me with huge, trusting eyes, as if asking whether it's safe to come down yet.

My own eyes are swimming.

Don't shoot. Don't shoot. Don't shoot.

The words ricochet in my head, above the ringing in my ears.

There's no other option.

But there is. If I was willing to stay, I could save her. Maybe not all the bears, but at least Hazel. The two of us could bushwhack our way through the peaks, meet up with Mom and Dad and Walt somewhere. We could manage it.

That's not what I want.

Don't shoot. Don't shoot. Don't shoot.

Gritting my teeth, bracing the butt against my already-bruised shoulder. I squeeze my eyes clear.

"Fucking prick," Walt yells behind me.

I pull the trigger.

Hazel falls with a muffled whomp and I hear myself cry out. Maybe it's only inside my head, but it sounds like the bleat that Hazel made when Dad first pulled her from his jacket.

Around me, the world goes still and silent. I drop to my knees beside my bear. I hurt as if it's me who's been shot. As if there's a giant, gaping hole through my chest.

After a while, I feel a hand on my back. Judith.

"We're going," she says.

My ears are mostly working again. If not my brain.

"I'll come. I'll help with the trip." I wipe my sleeve across my face.

She shakes her head. "Dad says if you're going to live in town, it's best you don't know where we are."

Another shot to the chest. I'm the one who told. I can't be trusted.

She leans down, squeezes my shoulders and kisses my cheek. Then she takes the rifle from beside me and presses her bus key into my hand.

A minute later, Mom hugs me.

Dad and Walt don't say goodbye.

17

I'm slumped beside Hazel, petting the soft, short hair of her snout, when the police and conservation officers show up. I smell their approach — a waft of ripening bud as they check out our plants. Then I watch as they circle the cabin, creeping forward, guns drawn. They crouch near the stoop, pound on the door and shout.

It's a conservation officer who spots me first. Which is lucky, I suppose. I can't take any more gunshots today. But a nice tranquilizer dart...

The officer notifies the cops, and the cops aren't exactly gentle. Efficient, yes, but not gentle.

"Who else is on the property?"

"He's unarmed."

"Are there other animals?"

"Outbuildings are clear."

"Do you know who did this?"

"Were these your bears?" The woman's voice is stern but calm. Maybe that's why it penetrates. Or maybe because I'm pressed into the ground, a knee against my back.

"Only Hazel," I say.

When they start to pull me up, I come face to face with

my bear again. I turn my head to the side as my stomach heaves. Black boots jump away just in time.

What did Hazel do to deserve this? She didn't understand, even after Walt and I pointed our guns. She thought she was a human. If strangers had approached, she would have trundled over to meet them, the way she approached Sam on the trail that day.

I shot her. She must have been so confused. She was waiting for me to save her.

I crumble. Choosing to leave the grow, breaking up with Sam, betraying Dad, the dead bears, my family — where the hell is my family? — everything comes out in shaking, choking sobs.

There are softer voices now. Apparently a puking, wheezing, snot-dripping teenager is not such a threat. There's a hand on my arm and I let myself be pulled up and led to a stump nearby.

I try to focus on the constable who squats in front of me. I make myself look only at her, concentrate on her face and block the bears from my peripheral vision. Block the image of Big Bugger who lies sprawled on the dirt like a trophy rug. Block the other uniforms.

This officer is about forty. She has brown hair pulled tight beneath her cap. Sweat stains show at the edges of her bullet-proof vest. She wears a belt hung heavy with baton and handcuffs and gun.

"Is Hazel your sister?" she asks.

I almost start bawling again like a little kid, but I hold it together. "Hazel's my bear."

Was. Hazel *was* my bear.

Bear gone. Family gone. Cabin swarming with cops. Everything gone.

"We have wildlife control officers here, because we heard the bears were habituated," the officer says.

Habituated to me.

"Who else are you concerned about?" she asks.

I almost tell her. But my thoughts start lining up slowly.

She's fishing for information, which means they don't know who was here. Which means my family likely made it safely to the campground.

Keep your head down. Maybe I haven't paid much attention to Dad's rule for the past few months, but I'm sure as hell going to follow it now.

I clamp my lips securely shut.

I see Sam's dad then, standing near the cabin, looking at me like I'm dirt.

I've lost my family, Hazel, Sam. But he doesn't care. He scribbles something on a notepad, then points an officer in a different direction. I wonder how I appear in his notes. "Witness" or "suspect" or "perpetrator."

Or "shitrat."

The officer beside me is still talking, her voice soothing.

"We could help each other find them," she says. "Your family must be close by."

The cops have been watching from the base of the mountain. Maybe they've skirted the boundaries of our grow. Maybe they even saw into the clearing from above. But they can't prove who lived here. It was almost always me going up and down the trail. If we were careful enough, they can't even prove a link between our cabin and the crop.

This place? Just a little summer camp. Our official address is the orchard where Judith's bus sits. Besides, Dad has a bad back. Walt's senile. My mom and I know nothing about those plants. Strangers must have snuck into the woods near our cabin and left drugs in hidden corners.

That was always supposed to be our story.

"I can't help you," I tell the officer.

The police drive me to the station and interview me, asking the same questions over and over, learning nothing.

I'm a minor. That's what saves me. There are rules about how long they can question me. After I call my dad's lawyer, there aren't any questions at all. Mr. Higgens appears briefly at the station and meets with me long enough to ask if I have somewhere to stay. Then the police release me, and I head straight for my sister's place.

Not a trace of Garrett's cologne. All I can smell when I pull open the door is Judith. She's there in the empty coffee cup in the sink, in the sweater thrown on the bench seat. When I lie on the bed, I can smell her on the pillow. It's as if I'm back in the lean-to, ten years old, waiting to build a fort, not worried about cops or crazed boyfriends or anything else, ever.

I curl into a fetal position on her bed. Images of Mom, Dad, Walt, Judith, Hazel and Sam swirl in my head, but eventually I sleep.

I sleep for what feels like days, until hunger and the smell of my own sweat force me up.

Then my cheese sandwich reminds me of Judith, and a spot of blood on my sleeve reminds me of Hazel, and it takes another few hours to pull myself together.

When I finally stumble outside, I've lost a day and a half. It's mid-morning and obscenely bright outside. A tractor mows swaths between the orchard trees and the breeze carries a hint of gasoline.

I text my motorcycle-riding contact, and it's not long before he roars down the orchard drive. We stand outside the bus.

"So," he says. "Trouble."

I grunt in agreement. "Dad might start again, but it'll take him a season or two to set up."

It's his turn to grunt. Then: "Anyone in town we need to worry about?"

I've thought about this part.

"A guy named Garrett," I say. "He works at the brewery. Office job of some sort."

It's not right, I know. But I don't feel even a tiny bit bad about it.

"No problem." The guy takes my forearm instead of my hand and pulls me close in a one-armed hug. Gives me a slap on the back. "I'll see you around," he says.

But I doubt I'll see him again. I'll never see Garrett, either. I assume he'll leave town. That's what I would do, if this guy and his friends came looking for me.

•

My second meeting is a little more official.

"Mr. Mawson," the lawyer says, leaning back in his leather chair and crossing his legs. He wears dark gray slacks with perfectly pressed seams. "What can I do for you?"

Even before I ask, I can tell he won't help me. He has the blank, closed face of a person who knows too many secrets.

Still, I have to ask.

"I was hoping you might give me a list of my family's real estate." I couldn't visit right away. But Judith went back and forth sometimes. I don't see why I couldn't occasionally…

Mr. Higgens swivels his chair to face me directly. "You know your dad has a property here in town."

I nod. That's the lot where Judith's bus sits, the trees around it rented to the family who owns the adjacent orchard.

"The remaining properties are in your grandfather's name, and I'm afraid I'm not at liberty to disclose that list."

I realize I've crossed my legs in a reflection of the lawyer. I uncross them, then press my fingers to my forehead. I have to decide how much to tell.

"They've moved from the place we were living," I say finally. "I want to make sure they're safe."

His forehead wrinkles. "What about your safety?"

"I'm almost eighteen."

"Old enough to look after yourself."

Obviously. I nod.

"If you were younger, we'd need to talk about foster care. But you're beyond that, son. As a formality, I've signed on as your guardian."

I scowl. "So that's it? Formalities?"

"Well, I'm not going to release a list of Walter's holdings," he says.

I feel like pounding on the desk. He knows where they are and he won't tell me.

But before I can consider my next move, he uncrosses his legs and scoots his chair forward. He leans his elbows on the desk.

"I've known your grandfather for a long time."

Long enough to know that Walt likes his privacy. Fucking prick.

"Longer than you might think. We went to Colombia together with the Peace Corps."

I blink at him. I had no idea Walt was with the Peace Corps. I'm not even completely clear on what the Peace Corps does.

"I crossed the border to Canada after I got my draft card in '70, same as Walt. He crossed the border a year after me. Joined the community I'd started north of Nelson. We tried to put our Colombia skills to use. When that dream broke up, though, we went different ways."

He tilts back in his chair, staring at the wall above my head. Maybe's he's back in his bell-bottoms, smoking up and playing Bob Dylan on a beat-up guitar.

"Has your grandpa told you much about it?" Mr. Higgens asks.

I shake my head.

"Up to forty thousand of us crossed the border. They don't know how many, exactly, because they didn't ask whether we'd just been drafted or if we were already soldiers. They didn't want to know."

When he lets his eyes settle on mine, I nod. I'm still trying to imagine him and Walt as friends.

"I suppose what I'm saying is that I'd do a lot for your grandfather."

"You'd be helping him by pointing me in the right direction."

He shakes his head. "Wouldn't even be legal."

Which seems a strange argument for a pot-smoking, commune-founding draft dodger to be making.

"I can do something different for you, though," he says. Then he punches a button on his phone and asks his secretary for a file. "Your dad has funds you can access."

Once his secretary has passed him a bundle of multicolored folders, he flips through. He begins laying papers in front of me. There's a bank statement, which I recognize. There's also an investment summary, which makes my eyes go wide, and a property assessment on the orchard.

"The investments are meant for you and your sister," he says. "They've been fairly lucrative over the years, and your family has added to them regularly. Rather a profitable business."

I manage to nod. The balance on those investments is big. Ridiculously big. Enough to pay for art school, or put a down payment on a house.

"Why didn't Judith…"

"She moved into town last year, I believe," the lawyer says. "Your dad visited then, and had me arrange for her to use the orchard property. He also covered her tuition. Your dad put these holdings jointly in your name and his. Still, I believe he would have released more to her eventually."

He holds my gaze again. "In his place, as a father, I would want to make sure my child was on track before I dumped a load of money in his lap."

He's talking about me now, not Judith.

"Do you have plans for your future, Isaac? School, perhaps?"

I struggle to make my brain form syllables. "Art school, maybe. I thought I'd work for a year first. For tuition."

Though that's hardly necessary now.

For the first time, Mr. Higgens smiles. He has a surprisingly kind smile, one that crinkles the corners of his eyes.

"You have Walter's genes."

He stares at the corner again for a while, like he's back in free-love land.

"We had a good friend in our first community, a man named George Ibitson. Maybe you've heard of him?"

Even as I'm shaking my head, a flash of memory surfaces. Walt's mouth working, struggling to form words after he looked at the book of my paintings. "George…Ib…" And when I think about it, the name does sound familiar. Landscapes, I think. Deserts and canyons.

"He moved back to San Francisco years ago," Mr. Higgens says. "Quite well known now, as an artist and as a teacher."

He checks his watch. "I have another appointment, I'm afraid." He looks sincerely sorry, and he comes around the desk to shake my hand. "You think about it and let me know what you'd like to do. Do you need access to some cash in the meantime?"

When I nod, he asks his secretary to make arrangements.

Then somehow I'm on the sidewalk outside, blinking in bright July sunshine.

I start walking. Then I start laughing. By the time I get to the bank, I'm laughing hard enough that people are giving me a wide berth on the sidewalk. I sink down onto a bench and try to regain control.

"Fucking prick." I shake my head, still catching my breath.

An old woman glares at me as she passes.

I don't even know who I'm swearing at. My dad, for hiding all this from me. Walt, for making it impossible for me to find them. Myself, for being generally stupid.

I knew what those plants were worth. Why did I never wonder where the money went? Why didn't I listen more patiently to Walt when he tried to tell me about his pot-smoking painter friend?

George Ibitson. Fucking prick.

None of this takes the sting out of things. It isn't as if I can plaster hundred-dollar bills over all my bullet holes. But at least it gives me focus.

I think of the painting I made of the fire-ravaged woods with the magenta fireweed bursting from the foreground. That's really what happens after forest fires. I've seen places on the mountain where lightning has ignited the trees and a patch of forest has burned black, crumpled into a charred bowl of ashes. It lasts only a season. By the following spring, there are greens growing from the dead logs and fireweed blooming in the gaps.

I want to tell Judith about the money. I want to tell Mom that everything's going to be okay. I want to tell Dad that I don't love art more than I love him, and tell Walt that I love art more than I love almost anything.

But I don't know where they are, if they've made it to the new cabin, if there was even a cabin waiting for them.

They're doing it all without me.

Which leaves me to do it all without them.

•

A couple of weeks later, Lucas slams the hood of the bus and leans against it. He's spent plenty of days in the orchard lately, getting my new home in running condition.

"Listen, we gotta talk about something," he says.

I'm a little surprised. He's been tinkering while I've been painting the bus, and we've been talking the whole time. I've already spilled my guts about the bears, and about my family's move to places unknown.

"That night we got pulled over. The night your sister came to get me," Lucas says, staring over my shoulder at the apple trees. "I told the police."

Slowly, his words penetrate.

"Told them what?"

"That you had a grow. And I told them where you lived."

I want to make him shut up.

"You don't even know where I lived."

"At first all their questions were about the truck and why we stole it. But a few minutes later, the questions became all about you. And they got really specific. Was your place north or south of the campground? Who lived with you? How long had you been there?"

He stops to scrub a hand through his hair. "Listen, I figured Sam had told them. She must have. They were looking for confirmation, so I gave it to them. In between begging them not to call my dad."

Looking at Lucas is like looking at someone years younger than me. He leaves for university soon. All he wants to do is please his folks, smooth out the rough edges in his life, do what everyone expects of him.

Was I like that once? And was it only a few weeks ago? It feels like decades.

"What exactly did you say?"

"That you lived above the campground somewhere, I didn't know what direction. I told them about the druid, the bear and the pot. They said otherwise I'd be arrested, and they'd be calling my parents, so I basically told them everything I could think of, which wasn't much..." He shakes his head. "I should have denied it. I could have told them nothing. Maybe they wouldn't have come."

I shake my head. I don't have the energy to get mad anymore, and I can't stand the thought of losing Lucas after everything else.

"It's not your fault. If I'd been careful enough, you wouldn't have known any of that stuff. And if Sam hadn't taken us on her crazy joyride, you wouldn't have found yourself at the station."

I can't say her name without an edge of bitterness creeping in, even though Sam's long gone. She had to cancel her drama-camp plans. Her dad sent her to stay with her grandma in Kamloops for the summer, and apparently Corporal Ko has applied for a transfer.

Lucas leaves for university soon.

"I guess you've worked off your debts anyway." I rap my knuckles against the bus. The Art Bus, we've dubbed it.

He grins. "I've got this baby running like a dream now."

"San Fran, here I come."

"You free to leave?"

I nod. "The crown decided last week not to press charges."

Back in July, Mr. Higgens said I was too young and too stupid to be charged with cultivation, or even with feeding dangerous animals. He said there wasn't enough proof, and it turns out he was right.

Lucas gathers his tools, but he stops to glance at the bus one last time.

"This is quite an accomplishment," he says. He gives me a hug before he leaves, slapping both hands on my back.

Then he's gone.

I step back to examine the work I touched up this morning.

Quite an accomplishment.

Hopefully it's enough. I looked up Walt's old friend, George Ibitson. He teaches private classes. All you have to do is submit a project for consideration.

Or, in my case, a bus.

On the left side I've painted the cabin — the same composition I used in last year's canvas, the one Mr. Pires submitted to the magazine. Mr. Pires has been to the orchard a couple of times, actually, offering a few pointers.

I circle to the far side of the bus, where I've painted the town of Creston, rising above patchwork fields. Everything's there: brewery, orchard, school, Sam's house, Canyon Street. Even the stolen pickup is hidden along a side road.

But the work I'm most proud of waits at the front. The hood of the school bus.

I stop when I get there and reach up my hand. I run my fingers over the fur, feeling the texture of the paint.

It's Hazel, running the way she did when she was half-grown, purely for the joy of it.

She looks like she's going to leap right off the metal.

She would, too. Then she'd be right alongside me, anywhere I decided to drive.

Thank you to the BC Arts Council for its financial support during the writing of this book.

I owe a huge thanks to Shelley Tanaka and Groundwood Books for falling in love with Hazel. For reading multiple drafts, my endless gratitude to my agent Amy Tompkins and to fellow writers Rachelle Delaney, Kallie George, Christy Goerzen, Stacey Matson, Lori Sherritt-Fleming and Maryn Quarless. Shannon Ozirny, you have amazing psychic powers.

Gordon and Shirley Lloyd and Sandy and Jason Racz read early drafts and continued to love me despite my incompetence. Min, Julia and Matthew managed to survive living with me through rewrites and revisions. You are all awesome.

For help with Isaac's homework, thank you to Michael Ward, professor and neighbor extraordinaire, who tells me that the answers are 4 and 2...unless I've misinterpreted the questions. Again.

Finally, a big thank-you to those friends and family members who would prefer not to be named but happen to have expertise in the growing of marijuana, the keeping of bears and the design of squatters' cabins in the woods.

Tanya Lloyd Kyi is the author of more than twenty books for young readers, including *Eyes and Spies* and *Anywhere but Here.* She spent several childhood years in Crawford Bay near Isaac's imaginary home, and while she didn't live on a grow-op, there were plenty of habituated bears around. She has yet to forgive the one that wrecked her swing set.

Tanya now lives in Vancouver with her husband and two children.